GASTON LE DOG

For Emile,
remembering with great fondness those long hot summers
when you were very young and you would ask me again
and again to tell you another "Gaston story",
lots of love, Dad.
M.R.

For my dad.
V.S.

First published 2023 by Walker Books Ltd
87 Vauxhall Walk, London SE11 5HJ

2 4 6 8 10 9 7 5 3 1

Text © 2023 Michael Rosen
Illustrations © 2023 Viviane Schwarz

The right of Michael Rosen and Viviane Schwarz to be identified as author and illustrator respectively of this work has been asserted in accordance with the Copyright, Designs and Patents Act 1988

This book has been typeset in Arvo

Printed and bound by CPI Group (UK) Ltd, Croydon CR0 4YY

British Library Cataloguing in Publication Data: a catalogue
record for this book is available from the British Library

ISBN 978-1-5295-0120-9
www.walker.co.uk

MIX
Paper from
responsible sources
FSC® C171272

THE INCREDIBLE ADVENTURES OF

GASTON LE DOG

Michael Rosen

illustrated by
Viviane Schwarz

WALKER
BOOKS

CHAPTER 1

In which I tell you about the lovely life I used to live and a desperate urge I had to go somewhere else.

I'**m a dog** who's done some amazing things in my time, you know. I'm Gaston le Dog.

Years ago, here in France, I lived in that barn over there. I was happy in there and I had good friends. Down on the ground there were the Mice. We'd have fun chasing each other all over the place. Up in the roof, there was Bat, clinging on to the tiles. And then, one summer, House Martin arrived. She made her nest out of mud, flying in and out of that open stone window you can see there. The Mice – we call them Souris. Bat – we call him Chauve-Souris – a bald mouse! Fancy that! The Mice thought that was very funny. House Martin, well, we call her Hirondelle de Fenêtre, but usually just Hirondelle.

Hirondelle was my best friend here. She was so kind and caring. You see I don't like flies – mouches. I don't like the way they come buzzing round my eyes and mouth. Lovely Hirondelle would say, "Don't worry, Gaston, I will swoop to and fro near you and I will catch those flies and they won't bother you any more."

That was nice of her, don't you think?

Sometimes, wasps – guêpes – flew in, and I didn't like them either. They didn't mean me any harm but if by mistake I bumped into one of them, they'd get angry and try to sting me. I don't like that. I don't like that at all.

Again, lovely Hirondelle would say, "Don't worry Gaston, I will swoop down and catch the wasps and they won't bother you any more."

Ha! That was good of her as well.

And once or twice, and this is the worst, hornets – frelons – would fly in. For some reason, my barn was on a route that hornets liked. Late at night, I'd hear a far-off rumble, sounding something like an old aeroplane, getting nearer and nearer. Then into the barn a hornet flew till it hit a beam. At that, it would start to chew the beam! Really! You could hear the sound as it nibbled away: *pikk-pikk-pikk*.

But sometimes the hornet missed the beam and hit me instead! Now, I don't know if you know, but hornets have a big, bad sting, and one thing you don't want to do to a hornet is make it cross. For one, it might hurt. For another, a hornet is so clever that when it gets cross, it makes a kind of perfume that, when other hornets smell it, they come flying over to see what's bothering the

first hornet. If you're not careful, you can have a whole host of them on to you. Some nights, I was worried that as I dozed off, a hornet would fly in through the open window and hit me.

But my lovely Hirondelle, she said, "Don't you worry about hornets, Gaston! While you're asleep, I'm wide awake on a beam, keeping an eye out. I'll swoop across when a hornet gets in. My shadow is enough to send it away. You won't be bothered by it ever again."

You see how she was? Just as I said, so kind.

I wanted to do kind things for her too, but it's not easy thinking of kind things for a house martin. In the end, she said that the kindest thing I could do was sleep near her house, because it brought the flies near by. And there was nothing she liked more than having flies to eat.

So, we got along well. Life was good.

But then – I don't know what it was. Call it a question, if you like. Or call it a voice in my ear, perhaps.

Let me explain. You see, many, many years earlier I had once been to the seaside. I remembered there was a beautiful beach; a beautiful, beautiful, beautiful beach, with yellowy-white sand that stretched for miles beside a beautiful blue sea. And there were sand-dunes, little hills of sand at the side of the beach, where I scampered up and down, running and chasing. I loved that. Someone was throwing a ball, and I chased after it, with my fast young legs, fetching and carrying, again and again.

It was so lovely that there was this moment, in the barn, when it suddenly came to me: I want to see that beach again. I want to see that beautiful blue sea again. It was as if the beach and the sea were calling to me ... calling to me ... calling to me.

Sometimes, I would come out of the barn, come into this field, up that little slope and sniff the air – *sniff, sniff, sniff* – and I would smell the sea. Or I thought I could. I would breathe it in and I could see the sea in my mind, and remember that delicious day on the beach and the dunes from long, long ago.

And I wanted to go back. I started to want to go back more than anything else in the world.

But how could I leave my lovely friend, Hirondelle?

I started to make up a speech I could give to her, to explain what I wanted to do.

"The thing is, Hirondelle," I would say to myself, "I have to follow my nose. I can feel the seaside calling me. Every day I get a tiny, tiny whiff of the salt water and picture the gulls circling in the sky, the blue waves topped with little white curls, the hot yellow sand, the curving sand-dunes and me chasing along... It's like a heaven that I just have to see. And the thing is, Hirondelle," I would say, "I won't be gone long. I promise, I promise, I promise. It can't be far. I'll hurry along – because as you know, I can hurry if I want to. I'll spend a few minutes there and then come hurrying back. And everything will be just as it was."

I practised this speech in my mind. Over and over again, till I was sure that I knew it off by heart. Then one night, just before I settled down in the corner of the barn,

...h, just as I had learned it.

...stened and listened. All the way through.

...Very well. I can see, Gaston, this matters to

...ian anything else in the whole world. If you don't

...il eat you up: you will become sad. And then sadder and sadder, till you won't even be able to get up in the morning. And if I said, 'No, don't go, don't leave me', you would blame me. You would say that I had stopped you doing the one thing you wanted to do most. You have to go. To tell you the truth, I know what it feels like to be far, far from home and..."

But I'm very sorry to say, I interrupted her and I blurted out, "That's so kind. Thank you." And I didn't ever hear what she was going to say. Instead I dived in with, "But how will you manage for flies?"

"Oh, don't you worry about that," she said. "I get about. I can always find flies. As I swoop and swerve about, I find flies. I'll be all right, believe me. Swooping and swerving..."

"Very well," I said. And I felt good that she was so sure that everything would be fine for her. I straightened myself out and said, "I will go first thing in the morning. I wouldn't be surprised if I was back by the evening. Or perhaps by the next day."

"Yes, mmm, yes," Hirondelle said in a voice that sounded just a bit doubtful. That "mmm". I heard it in my head over and over again.

CHAPTER 2

In which I tell you about who I met at the beginning of my journey.

In the morning, the very, very, very early morning, while it was still just a bit dark, while the sun wasn't even ready to peep over the end of the field and the air was fresh, I got up to go in search of the beach.

I put my head out of the barn, and everything smelled new.

"Goodbye, dear Hirondelle," I whispered.

"Goodbye, dear Gaston," she said. "See you soon."

"Yes indeed," I said. "I'll be back soon."

And I trotted out the door and into the field. I glanced back over my shoulder. For a moment I wondered whether I really should go. What if something bad happened to Hirondelle, and I wasn't there to help? But the sea was calling me and I put my head and my nose in front of me and got going.

I was only a few paces away from the barn when I heard a scratchy, crinkly noise in the grass.

"Hey Gaston," a voice said, "is that you?"

"It's me," I said. "Gaston le Dog. Who's that?"

"Me!" said the voice in a snorty, snuffly way.

I looked down and I could see it was Hérisson le Hedgehog.

He snorted again.

"Did you just burp?" I said.

"No," said Hérisson. "Well, yes."

"I thought so," I said. "It's OK, I don't mind."

"Where are you going?" Hérisson asked. "You're not usually up at this time."

"I'm going to the beach," I said.

Hérisson snorted again.

"Did you just burp again?"

"No!" he said. He sounded cross this time. "I did not. I snorted. It's what I do. I snort. But it was my way of saying, 'The beach? The beach? How do you think you're going to get to the beach? And what do you want to go there for anyway? Aren't you just fine where you are in your barn with your mates Bat, the Mice, Hirondelle? The beach is miles away, isn't it?'"

"Did your snorty noise mean all that?" I said.

"Yep," said Hérisson.

"Well," I said, "it's just something that I have to do. Call it hunting my dream. But hey, I can't hang about here talking to you or I'll never get going. I want to get to the beach and back today, so I can get back to the barn and my dear friend Hirondelle."

"The beach, you say," said Hérisson. "La plage."

He said the word in a lovely, spongey sort of a way, that made it sound all the more beautiful. *La plage*. It soothed me just to hear it.

"Yes!" I said. "I told you!"

"Won't you be... Won't you be a bit lonely?" Hérisson said.

I paused for a moment. I hadn't thought about that. Here I was whooshing off in a rush, and being lonely just hadn't crossed my mind.

"I don't suppose so," I said. "I mean, I don't know if I suppose so."

"Well," said Hérisson, "I don't want to go on any kind of

long journey. And I certainly don't want to go to some old beach, full of sand. But if you thought you might get a bit lonely on the way, I wouldn't mind, you know, giving you a bit of company. If you wanted. If you like."

I looked at Hérisson. Hérisson looked at me. I looked at his little legs and I thought of them running along beside me. I was just about to say, "It might be far" or "I'm not sure that you'll be able to keep up", when I looked into his eyes and I saw something.

Do you know what he was saying? He was actually begging me to take him with me. He couldn't say that he really, really, really wanted to come, because mostly he just snuffled and snorted. But I could see it.

"Do you know what?" I said. "It would be great if you came to the beach with me. As we walk along, we can sing songs and look out for things. Are you good at looking out for things?"

"Oh, I'm terrific at looking out for things," said Hérisson in a very excited voice. "And when they're dangerous things, I roll up in a ball, with all my spikes pointing outwards, and the dangerous things just give up and go away."

"Oh," I said, "that's very useful because we might meet some dangerous things. If they're really dangerous they might stop us from getting to the beach."

"Like what?" asked Hérisson.

"Hornets," I said straightaway.

"Oh yes. Them," said Hérisson. "Frelons. Don't worry, Gaston. I'll deal with them."

I felt really very good when I heard that. I was glad that I had thought that it was a good idea to bring Hérisson along with me. (Or did he think that?)

"Very well, Hérisson, allons-y, let's go!"

And Hérisson made his snuffly, snorty noise, got his little legs pumping away underneath him, *patter*, *patter*, *patter*, and off we went.

~ CHAPTER 3 ~

In which I tell you about another friend.

I could see straightaway that Hérisson and I didn't walk in the same way. For every step that I took, Hérisson took about ten! I was strolling along and he was running along like he was on wheels: *patter, patter, patter*. And as he pattered along, he snorted and snuffled.

"Do you have to snort and snuffle like that?" I said.

"Yes," he said, and went on snorting and snuffling.

"I'd quite like it if you stopped—"

Just then, a voice from somewhere above my head called out, "Are you two all right?"

"What's that?" said Hérisson.

"I don't know," I said. "It's coming from up above somewhere."

"Hmmph!" he snorted. "I can't lift my head to look and see. I look down. Not up. The stuff I'm looking for is always down. No point in looking up. If I spent my time looking UP, I'd miss the good stuff that's DOWN."

"Yes," I said, "I get you. Well, I'll look up for you."

And I did.

There was a brightly coloured butterfly, dancing in the air.

"Who are you?" I said.

"I'm Papillon le Butterfly," she said. "Are you two OK?"

"What makes you think we're not?" said Hérisson, still staring down.

"You seemed to be getting cross with each other about something. Are you having an argument?"

"Yes," said Hérisson. "He was trying to get me to stop snorting and snuffling. And I was trying to tell him that snorting and snuffling is what I do. I don't tell him to stop wagging his tail, do I?"

"My tail," I said, "doesn't make any noise. It just waves about. If you don't want to look at it, you can look the other way. There's nothing I can do if you snort and snuffle. Wagging tails and snuffling are not the same thing."

"Well," said Hérisson, "you pant and gasp. Panting and gasping is like snorting and snuffling."

Papillon joined in. "That's a very good point," she said.

"And when you pant and gasp, your tongue comes out and lollops about on the side of your mouth," said Hérisson.

"There was no need to say that, though," Papillon said.

"Thank you," I said. "I like lolling my tongue," I added, "and it cools me down when I get hot."

"Well, what am I supposed to do when I get hot?" asked Hérisson.

I looked at Papillon. Papillon looked at me.

And we both started to speak at the same time: "I ... er ... don't..." "... er ... don't know."

The truth is, neither of us knew what to do if Hérisson got hot.

Then Papillon said, "I could make myself into a kind of fan. I could get up close to you and flap. Like this."

At that, Papillon floated down next to Hérisson and fluttered.

Hérisson stopped talking and after a bit, he sighed. "Ahhhhh." It wasn't a snort or a snuffle. It was definitely a sigh.

"That's very nice," he said. "That works. That really works. Thanks very much."

"I can't do it all the time, though," Papillon said. "I have to find flowers."

"Hmmph," Hérisson said. "That must be very hard. Most flowers are UP. Mostly I look DOWN."

I thought, I could help out here. I can see flowers from miles away. And smell them.

"I could do the flowers thing," I said. "See! Over there! There's a big red one."

"Is there? Is there really? This is fantastic!" And Papillon did a flutter-dance in the air. "So when Hérisson gets hot, I can do the flapping work. And when I need to find flowers, you tell me what you can see and smell."

"That works," said Hérisson. And for the first time, he stopped snorting and snuffling. But I didn't dare tell him he had, in case he started up again.

We had been standing in the same spot for a while now as we chatted away, which was all very well, but it wasn't getting us any nearer to the beach. So I said, "It's great we've got this plan about being hot, and it's great we've got this plan about finding flowers, but actually ... we're going somewhere and we've got to keep going or we won't get there."

"Where are you going?" Papillon said, sounding a bit sad that her new friends – us – were about to leave.

"The beach," said Hérisson.

"Are there flowers on the beach?" Papillon asked.

I looked back at my memory of the beach. Flowers? Hmmm… There were some little tiny whitish-yellowish flowers on the dunes where I did my chasing, but not actual real flowers on the actual real beach.

"Not really," I said.

"What's the point of a beach, then?" she said.

Hérisson and I went very quiet. Neither of us knew what to say. Neither of us knew what was the point of a beach. A beach just is a beach, I thought. I wasn't sure that it had a point.

"It's great for running about. And jumping," I said.

"Is it good for flying about?"

"Oh yes," I said, "very good."

"Good," she said. "I'll come."

Hérisson and I went quiet. We hadn't actually asked Papillon if she wanted to come – but now that she had said that she wanted to come, there wasn't really any way that we could say that she couldn't come. It would have been plain rude.

So off we went: Hérisson and me, and now Papillon, up in the sky above us … *flip-flap, flip-flap, flip-flap.*

CHAPTER 4

In which there is a big problem.

It felt good to be walking along, the three of us. It felt very good. Just as I was thinking this, Hérisson said something that surprised me. In fact, it shocked me.

"We've been here before," he said.

"Have we?" I said.

"Look!" he said, and pointed with his nose to some marks on the ground. "Is that us? Did our feet do that?"

I looked closely. Papillon looked too. There were some tiny marks. And there were some bigger marks.

"They could be marks we made," I said.

"What if someone else made those marks?" Papillon said.

"You mean there could be another Hérisson and another Gaston le Dog walking this way?" Hérisson said.

I felt very, very odd thinking about that. I imagined meeting them and wondered what it would be like to meet myself...

"We could hurry along and see if we could catch up with them," Papillon said.

"Wait!" I said. "I have another idea."

I lowered my nose down to the marks and took in a great big sniff. Straightaway, I got it.

"Yes, we did make these marks. I can smell me. And I can smell you, Hérisson."

"I don't smell," Hérisson said.

I tried to think of a nice way to answer that. But really there was no nice way of saying it.

"We all smell," I said. "It's what we do. We go about smelling. And leaving some smell behind us."

"What?" Papillon said. "In those marks?"

"Yes," I said.

At that, Hérisson pushed his nose into the marks and said, "Hmm, I can smell you, but I can't smell me. Like I said, I don't smell."

"You do," I said, "but it's all right. Really."

Hérisson was getting angry. His snuffles and snorts were getting louder. I really didn't want to annoy him.

Then Papillon said something that stopped us both.

"You know what this means?" she said. "We're lost. Totally and completely lost."

It all went quiet while we thought about that.

"We've been walking alongside a hedge and we didn't notice that the hedge has brought us back to the same spot. All we've done is walk round the edge of a field."

"The hedge edge," Hérisson said. "Stupid hedge."

"I don't think the hedge is stupid," Papillon said.

Then it went quiet again as we wondered who was to blame for us being lost. I sat down.

Things are not going well, I thought. We aren't getting to the beach. And what with one thing and another, I couldn't smell the sea any more. Maybe it was the hedge's fault. It was in the way. Being big.

Papillon spoke again. "Listen, boys. Do you know how to get to the sea? Do you know what goes to the sea?"

"Grass," Hérisson said. "We could follow the grass."

"Grass is everywhere, Hérisson," I said. "We can't go everywhere."

"Worms," Hérisson said. "We could follow worms." And he said the word "worms" in a way that made worms sound very tasty.

"Worms are everywhere, Hérisson," I said. "We can't go everywhere."

"Worms are nowhere-near-enough everywhere," he said.

Yes, I thought, he does think worms are very tasty.

"Rivers!" said Papillon. "Rivers go to the sea. And streams. And tiny trickles that go into streams. They all go to the sea."

"Great," I said, feeling much better at hearing this. "So all we have to do is follow the river, or the stream. Or the trickle."

"Yes! That's it!" Hérisson said.

Good. We've solved it, I thought. But then...

"One thing, Papillon," I said.

"Yes?" she said.

"I know all we have to do now is follow the river to the sea..."

"Or the stream. Or the trickle," Hérisson added.

"But where is the river?" I said.

"Or the stream. Or the trickle," Hérisson said.

Papillon looked at us. "There isn't a river here – no, don't say 'or a stream or a trickle', Hérisson," Papillon said, and before Hérisson could snort or snuffle, she added, "But all I have to do is fly, up, up, up into the air, higher and higher and higher till I see a river, and then I come down and we go to the river. You follow me. I will guide you."

"Oh, that's very good," Hérisson said. "That's very good. If I didn't spend all my time looking down, I might have thought of that."

"Never mind," Papillon said, "let's get on. Here I go!"

When she said that, she did one big extra flap, turned up towards the sky and flapped and flipped, *flip-flap*, *flip-flap*, *flip-flap*, up, up, up, higher and higher and higher...

"How's she getting on?" Hérisson asked.

"She's getting on really well," I said. "She's up. Really up."

Papillon was getting smaller and smaller.

"You don't think she'll get lost up there, do you?" Hérisson said.

"I don't know," I said. "I really don't know."

And now I was worried. If Papillon was lost, and we were lost, what would we do then?

~ CHAPTER 5 ~

In which we get very worried...

I **stared and stared** up into the sky till my eyes went blurry. Is that Papillon, I wondered?

"Can you see her?" Hérisson said.

"Maybe," I said, trying to sound hopeful. "Or it could be a leaf."

"Well, it won't be a worm," Hérisson said thoughtfully. "Because worms aren't UP. They're DOWN." He chuckled.

I went on staring. Could she have got lost up there? Or blown away in the wind?

Hérisson was snuffling more than snorting. Almost snivelling.

Then, out of the sky, there was Papillon. Yes, she was here, flip-flapping her way down and down and down towards us.

We waved to her.

Well, I did. Hérisson found waving rather hard so he walked round in a circle instead. It helped him think.

"Did you find the river?" I shouted as soon as Papillon got near enough for me to hear.

"Or a stream? Or a trickle?" Hérisson shouted too.

No answer came.

Papillon got nearer till there she was, right above us.

On and on she fell, till she flopped straight on to the ground next to us: *flip-flap FLOP!*

And there she lay. Quite still.

Hérisson and I stared at Papillon. Had she ... had she ... died? Had that great flight into the air so worn her out that she was now ... gone for ever?

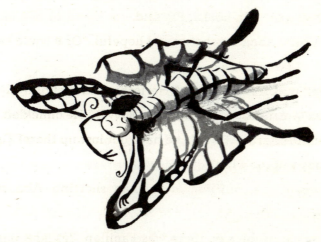

Lying there on the earth, she looked like a little coloured rag. A bit of rubbish that you might see by the side of the road. A sweet wrapper, perhaps.

We both put our noses close up to her.

"Papillon?" I said. "Papillon?"

No sound came.

"This is terrible," Hérisson said. "Utterly terrible."

I stared at Papillon, the little rag.

"Why don't you wag your tail near her?" Hérisson said. "It might give her more air."

So I did that. I stood and wagged my tail and it wafted cool air over her. At first there was nothing. Papillon was totally still.

But then, there was a tiny movement. A little ripple along Papillon's wing. Nothing more. Then another. And another.

We watched, hardly daring to believe what we could see. With a bit of a shake, Papillon got up on to one leg, then another, then another.

Now she was awake!

"Papillon!" shouted Hérisson. "You didn't die!"

"Nope," Papillon said. "I didn't die. You're right. I was just having a rest. It was a long hard trip and halfway down, I shut my eyes and I think I must have fallen asleep. I feel better now."

Amazing, I thought.

"It was incredible up there," Papillon said. "The things I could see: forests, mountains, towns far, far away in the distance, villages..."

"That's wonderful, Papillon," I said, "but while you were up there, did you see...?"

"...clouds, valleys ... the cows in the fields were like little dots..."

"Yes," I said, "but did you see a river?"

"Or a stream? Or a trickle?" Hérisson said.

"Oh no," Papillon said. "I was much too high up to see a stream or a trickle."

"But what about a river? Could you see a river?" I said.

She paused to think for a moment. "A river ... let me see... YES! I did see a river."

Hérisson and I cheered. "Hurrah!"

"So all we've got to do now," I said, "is go to the river and the river will take us to the sea. Is that right?"

"Yes, that's right," Papillon said. "But ... but ... there may be one or two..."

She faded out, not finishing what she was saying.

"One or two what?" I said.

"Oh, nothing much," she said. "There are always one or two somethings or other."

"Except worms," Hérisson said. "Sometimes there are no worms. Not even one or two."

I was wondering what Papillon meant but off we went. Papillon led the way because she knew where the river was. Well, we thought she did.

CHAPTER 6

In which we do find one or two things.

Papillon flew ahead of us, making sure we didn't do that following-the-hedge silliness again.

"I am so looking forward to this beach place," she said with a sigh, just as we came round the edge of a tree.

There in front of us was a huge wall. A wall

higher, wider and longer than I had ever seen before. It was right where we needed to go. And it was in the way. Very much in the way.

It was too high to climb. Too wide and too long to go round. It was also very shiny, so if I or Hérisson got it into our minds that we could have a go at climbing it, we had to get it out of our minds straightaway. We could have gone up it for a bit, but then we would have slid down again.

"It's not looking good, Gaston," Hérisson said.

"I know," I said. "Papillon, perhaps you could fly up and look over?"

"I'm too tired," said Papillon. "My flying-up muscles have given up for the day. Only my flying-along ones are working at the moment."

Just then, I heard a voice. It was coming from behind the wall.

"Come in, come in," it said in a buzzy, bossy sort of a way.

"We can't," I called out. "There's a wall."

"Ah, yes," said the voice. "You have to say the word."

"What word?" I said.

"The special word that opens the wall," came the reply.

"We don't know the special word," I said.

"Neither do I," said the voice.

That was a big puzzle. If we didn't know the word and the voice on the other side of the wall didn't know the word, we were ... er ... we were ... er ... stuck.

Hérisson was thinking hard. "We could try saying some words," he said, "and see if any of them work."

"You're saying words all the time," Papillon said. "And none of them are working."

"Yes," I said. "When you think about it, there are a lot of words, aren't there?"

"I am thinking about it," said Hérisson, a bit snappily. "Why don't we just try some and see what happens?"

Papillon said, "We could ask each other questions, like, 'Where do you most want to go?' or 'What's the tastiest thing you've ever eaten?'"

"Worms," said Hérisson.

We looked at the wall. It didn't move.

"No!" shouted the buzzy, bossy voice. "'Worms' hasn't done the job."

"They do the job for me," Hérisson said.

"What about your 'where do you most want to go?' question?" I said.

"The beach!" shouted Papillon, who was still resting her flying-up muscles.

The wall didn't move.

"'Beach' isn't right," shouted the buzzy, bossy voice.

The buzzy, bossy voice was starting to annoy me, but I tried to stay hopeful.

"What about those words you say about where you look?" I said to Hérisson. "Like 'UP' and 'DOWN'."

"UP!" he shouted. "DOWN!"

Nothing happened, apart from the buzzy, bossy voice saying "No!" over and over again.

He tried some more: "THROUGH! OVER! IN! OUT! UNDER!"

None of them worked either. I was getting desperate now. It was looking like we were stuck. And I wanted so much to get to the beach.

Then Papillon said, "What about things we don't want, or things we are scared of ... that sort of thing?"

"No, that won't work," said Hérisson. "The wall won't like it."

"I don't think the wall thinks like that," I said. "It's a wall."

"I know it's a wall," said Hérisson. "I've been thinking about walls for a long time. Broken walls sometimes have worms in them."

Papillon looked like she was thinking that we needed to get back on track with more words.

"What do you not want most of all?" she said.

"Thunder!" I shouted.

The wall didn't move.

"No," shouted the buzzy, bossy voice.

"Mud!" shouted Hérisson.

"Mud?" I said. "What's the matter with mud?"

"It gets in my prickles," he said.

"No!" shouted the buzzy, bossy voice.

"It does get in my prickles!" said Hérisson.

"No," I said, "the buzzy, bossy voice is saying that 'mud' is not the right word to open the wall."

"I'm not buzzy and bossy," the buzzy, bossy voice shouted.

Papillon said, "What about things we're scared of?" And answered her own question with, "Trumpets!"

"Why trumpets?" I asked.

"Too loud and too shiny," she said. "And I might fly into a trumpet and never get out."

"I couldn't fly into a trumpet," I said.

"No," shouted the buzzy, bossy voice.

"You're not helping," I shouted back.

"I know I'm not," shouted the buzzy, bossy voice.

"What about you two?" Papillon said to Hérisson and me.

Then something very strange happened. Both at the same time, we said, "Snakes!"

That was funny that we thought exactly the same thing.

We started laughing at this but then, at that very moment, the wall started moving. Well, part of it did. Near to where we were, one section slid slowly sideways. That was a bit of a shock.

I could see that behind the opening was a little grey door. On the door it said "Château Château". (That's "Castle Castle".)

Hmmm, that seemed silly. Why would anyone write "Château" twice? Underneath there was a kind of shield. On the shield there was a pair of boots.

"It's worked!" Papillon said, sounding happier than a grasshopper.

"Come in, come in," shouted the buzzy, bossy voice, so I pushed the little grey door, it opened, and in we went, all three of us.

There to meet us in the great big courtyard was the owner of the buzzy, bossy voice: Libellule la Dragonfly.

Château Château was very, very old, full of great grey towers and turrets, with the ground paved in grey stone. The windows were grey too.

"You're welcome," Libellule said. "Make yourself at home! The master loves people to come and stay. The trouble is no one seems to come these days."

Libellule's wings were beautiful and shimmered in the light. He seemed to know this and he made them shimmer all the time. He glanced at the wings as they shimmered, as if he was saying to himself, "Oh, look at my lovely shimmery wings."

"I'll tell you why no one comes these days," Hérisson said rather forcefully. "It's because you've got a great big wall and it's very, very hard to get it to open. If it wasn't for our friend Papillon thinking up ways for us to come up with the right word, we would never have got in."

"Look," Papillon said, "we don't want to stay, we're just passing through. We're going to the beach."

"Oh no," Libellule said, "you're staying. Now you're in, you're in."

At that, I heard the door shut behind us. All by itself.

Hérisson whispered to me, "I don't like this."

I whispered back, "Neither do I."

"What do we do now?" Hérisson whispered.

"I don't know," I whispered.

CHAPTER 7

In which things go wrong.

"**Follow me**," Libellule said, and he shimmered on ahead of us.

I was feeling worried. And sad. I was worried that we weren't getting to the beach. And not getting to the beach was also making me sad. Getting to the beach was all I wanted to do. Maybe we would see a way out of Château Château if we followed Libellule, so that's what we did.

He darted through a gateway, round a corner, up some steps, in through a door and then into a huge, huge, huge room, stretching way, way into the distance. It was dark and empty. Hanging from the ceiling were old flags and on the walls there were pictures of old men staring at us.

Libellule kept on flying ahead of us and after a short while, I started to make out something at the end of this hall. There was an old grey throne. Sitting on it was an old grey cat – Chat, as we say in French – wearing a crown and a pair of boots. His feet rested on a box. On the box it said "Treasure".

Hmmm, I thought. Treasure? Interesting!

"Some foolish creatures to see you, my lord," Libellule said.

I thought, that's not right. We didn't come to see this cat. We came in so we could get out.

Chat looked at us. He smiled in a tired sort of a way and then coughed. He leaned forward and said, "I will give you good things to eat and drink. You will be very happy here."

Now I was getting very worried. How long did this cat king creature think we were going to stay? I looked at Papillon and Hérisson. They were looking worried too.

"Before you have something to eat," Chat said with a strange smile on his face, "Libellule will show you to your room."

He gave a tired wave with his leg, coughed again and Libellule set off again, and we followed: out of the door, along a long, long passage with more pictures of old men on the walls, round a corner, up some stairs till we arrived at an old broken door.

"Push the door – you, the dog," Libellule said.

I did, the door opened, and in we went.

"I'll call you when supper is ready," he said, and he flew out of the room, shimmering all the while as if there was some kind of hidden light in his wings. As he flew out of the room, the door closed behind him, and the lock clicked. I went over to it and tried to open it. It was no good. I couldn't.

"Things are not going very well," Hérisson said carefully.

Papillon was flip-flapping about like she was hunting for a way out. The room was empty apart from one old tired bed and a small table with a candle on it. Just that. There were no windows. And the ceiling was high up, far, far away from us.

I sat down on the bed. How could things have gone so wrong?

"NOOOOOO!" screamed Hérisson, and rolled himself up into a ball.

Papillon flew straight up and landed on the tiniest of ledges between two of the stone bricks in the wall.

"What?" I said. "What's the matter?"

Papillon pointed to the corner of the room.

"What the matter with you two?" I said.

Then I looked closer at the corner. There, sliding towards me was ... a snake – Serpent le Snake.

Things had become very, very dangerous.

Well, not very dangerous for Papillon, because she was high up on the ledge. And not very dangerous for Hérisson, because he was curled up into a ball. But very dangerous for the other one among us – me.

"How did you get in?" Serpent said.

"We shouted 'snakes!'" I said.

"Why did you do that?" she said.

"Because Papillon asked us what we were most scared of," I said, trying very hard to tell the truth.

"That's where you went wrong," Serpent said.

"I know," I said, trying to work out if Serpent would climb up the leg of the bed to get to me. I went on, "If we hadn't said something together, the door wouldn't have opened in the wall and we wouldn't have ended up in this terrible place."

"No," she said, "I meant there's nothing to be scared of."

There was a muffled snorty sound coming from the ball that was Hérisson. Serpent slid over to him.

"Do you think I'm dangerous?"

Hérisson did the muffled snort again.

"I think he said, 'yes'," I said.

"I think so too," Papillon said from up on high.

"Why's that?" Serpent said in what was really not a very dangerous voice at all.

"*Ffffbbbb bbbffff fbfb*," Hérisson said.

"I think he said, 'You might bite us, poison us and eat us,'" I said, not knowing if he really did say that. I just said what I was thinking.

"Yes," Papillon called out.

"No, no, no," Serpent said in a kind way. "I don't do that sort of thing to creatures like you. Unless you tread on me. We can do a deal. You don't tread on me, and I won't bite you. What do you think?"

"Sounds very good to me," I said. "What do you think, Hérisson?"

"*Bfff bfff, fffbbb,*" Hérisson said.

"Now listen to me very carefully," Serpent said. "I know everything that goes on here. I know everything that's gone on here for years and years and years. If you do everything I say, you may get out of here alive and well. If you don't, I can't bear to think what might happen to you. Some visitors – before you – didn't do what I said, and things turned out very badly..."

I had a feeling that what she was saying was true, so I sat down on the bed and waited. Papillon stayed up on the wall and Hérisson stayed rolled up. They were being more careful than me. I wondered who was right. Me or them?

CHAPTER 8

In which we hear of bad things that happened before.

"**I**t's like this," Serpent began. "This place once used to be full of life and fun. Dancing and feasting. Music in the courtyard. Jesters, jugglers, puppet shows and plays. That was back in the days of the Marquis de Carabas and his wife, Princesse la Princess. Their servant was Chat le Cat, a famous cat who ran the place. He ran about making sure that everything was done right: the cooking, the cleaning, the woodcutting, the milking, the bread-making, making the fires in winter, fetching water … all of it, he made sure that people did it.

"But he was cruel. If people didn't do what he said, he'd snarl and scratch and bite. People were afraid of him, even though he was just a cat. You see, they had heard that he had special powers: special powers that he had got from something that happened a long time ago. You see, I know everything!

"Once upon a time in this place, there lived an Ogre, a gross and horrible monster who had the special power of being able to turn himself into anything he wanted – an even bigger monster, or a giant, a bull, a fly or a pigeon – anything! One day, Chat came here and met the Ogre. The Ogre roared and shouted at the cat and told him that he could turn himself into anything he wanted, so Chat said, 'I don't believe you. I bet you can't turn yourself into a mouse.'

"'Oh yes I can,' bellowed the Ogre, and he turned himself into a mouse. Do you know what happened next?"

Papillon called out from the ledge, "The cat ate the mouse."

"Yes," Serpent said. "How did you know?"

"Oh, I think someone told me this story," she said. "It's called Puss in Boots. The Marquis started out life as a miller's son, didn't he? And only became a Marquis when the cat ate the Ogre and gave the Château to the miller's son."

"Hang on," Serpent said, "who's telling the story here?"

"All right, carry on!"

Serpent went on: "The secret that people whispered to each other afterwards was that Chat le Cat had got the power of being able to turn anybody into anything – himself or anyone else – and he'd got this power from the Ogre, by eating the Ogre! And that's why everyone became so afraid of the cat. Everyone thought that one day, he might turn himself into an ogre or a crocodile or even a snake.

"People don't like to be afraid, so they started drifting away from here: the people who looked after the cows, the people who fetched the water, the people who cooked in the kitchen, who cut the wood, or who worked in the mill... Bit by bit, one by one, they drifted away.

"The Marquis de Carabas and Princesse la Princess couldn't figure out what was going on. Why was everything going wrong? They asked Chat and he said he didn't know – but of course he did. But he didn't tell them. Instead, he got angrier and angrier and nastier and nastier and greedier and greedier.

"He plotted. How could he get rid of the Marquis and Princesse? But you don't want to know that, do you?"

"*Fbbb bbfffbbb bfbfbfbf,*" Hérisson said.

"He says he would," I said.

"Well let me have a bit of a stretch, and then I'll carry on... You see," Serpent said, "in this Château, there was an old mill. A water mill. There's a river over there, and a big wheel. The water rushes past the wheel and makes it turn. That makes the big stone wheels inside turn, and they grind up the flour to make the bread."

"Oh no," Papillon said, jumping ahead in the story, "please don't say ... that the cat pushed the Marquis and Princesse into the—"

"Wait," said Serpent, "hang on there, Papillon. What happened is that Chat played a trick on them. He took them to the mill where the wheels grind together and the water rushes and rushes ... and sad to say, the Marquis and Princesse were never seen again."

Oh no, I thought, that's ghastly. Into my mind came a terrible picture.

"Well, now the cat had the Château all to himself. And as his name was Chat, he called the Château, 'Château Château'. It was his little joke. Though he was the only one who thought it was funny. And that's the thing. The last of the fun and laughter went.

"Now Chat had a problem. He couldn't get enough people to stay and do the work. So what he did next was use his powers to trap those who come by Château Château."

"You mean, like us?" Hérisson said.

"Yes," Serpent said.

"This all started out as a lovely, fun trip to the seaside, and now it's become a horror. A terrifying, awful trap," Papillon said.

"But you, you're all right," Hérisson said. "You can just flip-flap away."

"I could," Papillon replied, "but I won't. I'm going to stay with you. You might need me later to see things from up high like I did before."

I thought that was very nice of her and it cheered me up. "Thank you, Papillon."

Hérisson was doing some more thinking. "Are you saying that there are others here who came by Château Château, who came in and can't get out?"

"Yes," Serpent said.

"And they're still here?"

"Yes," she said, in a very serious way.

"And why are you here?" Papillon asked her.

"Because this is one of the best places on earth for what I want."

"What's that?" I said.

"Slugs and snails," she said. "There are cellars down below Château Château and they're damp and cold and full of slugs and snails. Ooooh, it's so lovely."

Hérisson looked interested. "And worms?" he asked.

"Yes," Serpent said.

"Now look here, Hérisson," I said, "don't start thinking you're going to stay here."

"No I wasn't, I wasn't, really I wasn't... But, Serpent," he said, "are there really worms down there?"

"Yes," Serpent said. "Now listen carefully you three. In a minute, Libellule is going to be back to take you down to eat. There will be sumptuous food. Food that you will want to eat more than anything in the world. But if you do, you will be turned into gnomes and be stuck here for ever. That's how the cat's magic works."

"What's a gnome?" Hérisson asked.

"A little painted stone man. I told you, Chat has the power to turn anyone into anything. So, you mustn't touch even the smallest crumb of what's given to you. If you can resist that food from the time it's served up on the table for seven days and seven nights, you'll break the power of the cat."

"But how? What's the way out?" I said.

"That's the problem," Serpent said. "The only way out is..."

But before she could finish, Libellule was back. When I looked round for Serpent, she had gone. She had heard Libellule before we did, and she had disappeared.

"Follow me," Libellule called out to us.

And we did, leaving Serpent behind.

CHAPTER 9

In which things start to get dangerous.

Libellule **shimmered ahead** of us down the passageways, all the way back to the great, grey hall.

"You may sit there, and there, and there," he said, buzzing over some places laid out for us on a great, grey table. "You, hedgehog thing, sit here," he said, buzzing at a plate full of worms and snails.

"You butterfly thing, sit here," he said, buzzing at a plate of flowers.

"And you, dog thing, sit here," he said, buzzing at a plate of bones. "It's all yours! Eat as much as you want, and his lordship, the great Chat himself, will be back to see you." And off shimmered Libellule.

We were on our own. With all that lovely delicious food. Oooh, it was tempting. I so, so, so wanted to get crunching on those bones. I looked at Hérisson. He was staring at the worms and shaking. He was so excited to see them there, right in front of him. And Papillon, she was flip-flapping and flitting and floating, and quivering to and fro over the flowers.

Hérisson whispered to me, "I think if I had just one bit of a worm, surely I wouldn't turn into a gnome..."

"No," said Papillon, "don't do it, Hérisson, don't do it."

I went on staring at the bones. I could imagine hearing the gorgeous crunch in my mouth that would come if I bit into that lovely little bone in front of me.

"You know what?" I said. "I think one little bone couldn't turn me into a gnome. I'm going to have just a tiny nibble."

"Don't do it! Don't do it," Papillon said, but even she was staring hard at a beautiful purple flower in the middle of her plate.

But we didn't listen, Hérisson and I. First Hérisson had the tiniest lick of a wriggly worm, then I flipped that little bone up off the plate and into my mouth...

And in less time than it takes to wag a tail, we started turning into little painted stone gnomes.

But Papillon didn't. She wasn't so foolish to poke her nose into that purple flower, even though she so, so, so wanted to. She watched with horror as now all she had as friends were two gnomes, each with silly smiley faces staring at her.

I looked down at myself. I was as gaudy as a roundabout at the fair. I could move – well, just about – in a clumsy, stumbling sort of a way. It was the same with Hérisson. We stared at each other, horrified to see what we had become. Then we looked at Papillon, still the butterfly she ever was. And look how clever she is, I thought to myself. She didn't eat anything. She did just as Serpent told us to. I felt such a fool.

Just then in came Chat le Cat. He wandered over to the table where we sat, two gnomes staring at our food.

"You won't need that now," he said, with a nasty little smile on his face. I noticed then, for the first time, that he had a bunch of keys tied to his belt and he liked to jingle them with his paw as he spoke.

He looked at the plate of flowers and Papillon. "What about you?" he said. "Won't you have a little poke around in any of those gorgeous flowers?"

Papillon flittered up in the air above us. Chat tried to grab her but she was too quick for him.

"Come on, butterfly," he said in a syrupy voice. "You know you want to."

Again Papillon said nothing, while we looked on, wondering if she too would give in and end up as a gnome. Then in shimmered Libellule.

"You two, come with me," he said, and I felt that whatever he said, I had to do it.

"Yes, sir," I said, and my voice came out sounding like an old man.

"Yes, sir," Hérisson said, his voice nearly the same.

And off we went down the passageways, following Libellule.

The sad thing is, I knew that we were leaving Papillon behind with that terrible cat but ... we couldn't do anything.

Then I saw where Libellule was taking us: to the mill!

Somewhere deep in my little stone brain, I could remember that we had been told that something bad had once happened at the mill... Would this happen to us too? Would we be thrown into the water? We were made of stone... We would sink ... like a stone!

~ CHAPTER 10 ~

In which we start to worry
we are stuck for ever.

Sure enough, Libellule took us to the mill, the very place that Serpent had told us about. And what a strange sight. In the room there were gnomes! Just like us! Two painted stone gnomes, lifting, pushing, pulling, dragging. The wheels were turning and turning. The two gnomes were doing the work to make the flour. But they were once creatures like us, who had got caught by Chat in his wicked Château Château. I wondered who they had been before they became gnomes...

Libellule pointed at a pile of huge, heavy sacks then buzzed towards a big cart, showing us that we had to lift the sacks on to a big hook on the end of a chain that seemed to come out of the sky.

Up went the chain out of sight, and somewhere – out there – someone took the sack and the hook came down and we started all over again.

So we joined the other two, working in the Château Château mill. Would it be for ever? Was this what had become of us? All I had wanted to do was go to the seaside, go to the beach and come home and tell Hirondelle all about it. All that seemed far, far away now. Places we would never ever go again.

No time to think of that. We had to keep on with the lifting and pulling and pushing. And the thing is, the old water wheel that used to turn and turn was broken. So now, we had to do the work to turn the wheels to grind the flour. Heavy, heavy work. For evermore.

Well, it would have been, if it wasn't for Papillon.

You remember, we left her behind in the hall, with Chat desperate to get her to have some nectar from the flowers. Somewhere in the back of my mind, I remembered that if Papillon refused to eat for seven days and seven nights, the power of the cat would be broken. But would she be able to? And even if she could, would we be stuck as little stone gnomes anyway? Horrible thought!

Once Libellule was sure that we had got down to work, he went off, shimmering as always.

I muttered at one of the gnomes, "What did you used to be?"

"I was Renard le Fox," she said.

"What about you?" I asked the other.

"I was Hibou le Owl," she said.

"And you ate something in the hall?" I said.

They nodded.

"Did no one warn you not to?" I said.

"No, not at all," Renard said.

"No," Hibou said sadly.

"Oh," I said. "We were warned, weren't we, Hérisson?"

He nodded.

"Then why in heaven's name did you eat something?" Renard said.

"It looked so, so, so delicious," Hérisson said.

But I felt so stupid that I hadn't listened to Serpent and done what she had said: not eat the bones, not even one tiny little one.

"The thing is," I said, "there's one more of us: Papillon. When we left the hall, she still hadn't eaten anything."

"Why does that matter?" Hibou said.

"Because if she can keep going, not eating anything for seven days and seven nights, it will break the power of the cat."

"Then what?" Renard asked.

And I didn't know what to say, because I didn't know.

"I don't know," I said. "Maybe Serpent knows..."

I told them all that I knew about Serpent and how she had tried to help us, but right now I didn't know where she was. Though I did wonder: maybe she was in the Château cellars looking for slugs and snails.

Then Libellule came back and we thought it best to stop talking and get on with the work. But all the time I was hoping that Papillon could hang on and not eat the flowers.

So it was that all four of us, the little painted stone gnomes, got on with the back-breaking work, for one day, two days, three days, four days, five days, six days ... and on to the seventh day.

What would happen at the end of the seventh night?

I wondered. If it was nothing, then I would know that Papillon had given in. She would have eaten some of the flowers, and we would be stuck in the mill for evermore.

All through the seventh day, all four of us looked at each other as we worked, turning the wheel, bagging the flour, lifting the sacks, pulling the carts. I looked at Libellule. Was he shimmering just a bit quicker today? Did he look just a tiny bit nervous

perhaps? Was that because he was worried that something big was going to happen? Maybe I was imagining it, just trying to be hopeful because I couldn't bear the thought of being stuck here for ever and ever.

I glanced out of the window. The sun was going down, the seventh day was coming to an end. One more night to get through and we'd see. Would Papillon be able to hold on and not eat anything?

It was a long, long night.

I kept getting up and looking out of the window, but it was always night, a night that went on for ever. I hunted the sky, looking for a sign of the sun rising. Would Papillon get through the night without eating?

Then I saw the faintest streak of light. The break before the break of dawn. I held my breath. Any moment now the seven days and seven nights would be over. Yes! There was the teeniest, tiniest tip of the sun peeping at me.

Well? I looked at the others. They looked at me.

Anything going to happen?

At that moment we heard a rumbling,

at first far off, but then nearer. The rumbling turned into a roar, and in the middle of the roar there was a cracking. We rushed to the other window and looked back at Château Château. It was breaking and crumbling. The great, grey castle was falling down. Down, down, down to the ground. Great clouds of dust flew up, and all the while, a sound of thunder. A great grim roar.

We looked at each other. We knew what this meant: Papillon had not eaten any flowers! She had resisted! The power of the cat was broken! Papillon had done it! All by herself!

But what was going to happen now? In a flash, I thought of first Papillon, then Serpent, then Chat himself and shimmering Libellule. What was going to happen to them? Where were they? And then I looked at us. Were we going to stay as silly little painted men?

Gnomes!

~ CHAPTER 11 ~

**In which things fall apart, but we wonder if
they might be stuck together again.**

But no. We too: we started to crack and break apart. Our
stony bodies began to fall off us in pieces, like eggshells.
We were like baby birds, stepping out of our gnome-shells
and then growing to be full-size: Renard le Fox, Hibou le Owl,
Hérisson le Hedgehog and me, Gaston le Dog. We looked
at each other and down at ourselves, making sure we really
were alive and back to who we were. We were!

All was fine, apart from wondering what had happened to Papillon. Brave Papillon, who had saved us from what would have been a terrible life. Then, through the cloud of dust that hung over the great grey Château Château, we saw a movement. Coming through the dust we saw the cat himself, Chat.

Oh no! Not him. I had hoped that maybe the castle had fallen on top of him and that would be that, the end of the cat! But no, here he was, dusting himself down, coughing and walking towards us, dragging his treasure box behind him, with the keys on his belt, jangling along as he walked.

I glanced at the treasure box. Hmm, I thought, there must be something very special in there if he's dragging it everywhere.

But where was Papillon?

I sat back, pulled back my lips and snarled at Chat. Renard snarled too. (Good snarling, Renard, I thought.) Hibou flew up on to a beam in the mill and Hérisson got ready to roll himself up in a ball. But me, *me*, up against a cat? I reckoned I could handle it on my own, thank you very much. *Snarl! Snarl! Snarl!*

The moment I did that, though, Chat pulled a white handkerchief out of his pocket and waved it. He waved it three times. I knew what that meant. He came in peace. He meant no harm. I stopped snarling and he came closer.

"It's over," he said. "The game's up. I'm just a cat now.

The magic is broken. My powers are finished. All I have are my whiskers, my boots and my little box. I'm still clever. I always was clever. But no magic left. All that magic I got from eating the Ogre has gone. I am Chat."

And he finished that speech with a rather nice little miaow.

We stared at him. One moment we were in the middle of the horror of a lifetime of work in the mill, and now we were free. Free to go wherever we wanted, however we wanted.

"Hérisson," I said, "you know what this means, don't you?"

"Yes," said Hérisson. "I could nip back to Château Château, look for those cellars Serpent talked about and get tucking into some slugs, snails and worms."

"And mice?" said Hibou.

"I don't know about mice," Hérisson said. "Serpent didn't say anything about mice."

Hibou looked sad and uttered a low "*hooo!*"

"But don't you see?" I said. "We're free to go to see the sea. It's what we were doing. Remember?"

"Oh yes," said Hérisson, but I don't think he thought that was better than going to look at the cellar.

"What's all this about the sea?" Renard chipped in.

"Yes," said Chat, "you didn't say anything about the sea."

"No," Hérisson said, "because first you locked us up, then you turned us into little gnomes."

"I know, I know, I know," said Chat. "And I'm sorry. Very, very, very sorry."

He hung his head down. Was he really, really sorry? I wondered.

"And ..." he said slowly, "if you're going to the seaside, do you think, do you think, I could ... come too? I can't stay here. Look at the place." He waved his hand in the direction of the rubble and dust. "I have a very bad chest."

He coughed and then went on.

"If I stayed here, I wouldn't survive. All that dust and grit. It would get into my lungs. I wouldn't last the winter."

I glanced at Renard and Hibou.

"What do you think, folks?" I said.

Hibou wasn't sure. Renard wasn't sure. Hérisson had an idea.

"You can come if you find Papillon. Papillon is our friend. We wouldn't even be talking about going to the seaside if it wasn't for her. And most of the time, I can't even see her." He turned to Renard. "I can't really look up. It's my neck. It doesn't bend up, you see."

"That's a good idea, Hérisson," I said, and turned to Chat. "Yes, if you can find our friend Papillon, you can come too."

"Fair enough," said Chat, "and you'll be glad you said that."

And he turned round, stuffed his hankie in his pocket and disappeared into the dust, still dragging his box.

"Oh no," Hérisson said, "we forgot to ask him about Serpent."

"Are you really friends with a snake?" Renard asked.

"Yes," I said. "We have a deal. So long as we don't tread on her, she's fine."

"Yes, where is she?" Hérisson asked as if he was worried about her, though I think the main reason was because he was still thinking about the cellar full of slugs and snails and worms.

"Are you coming too, Hibou?" Renard asked.

"What's the beach like at night?" Hibou asked. "I like the night."

I said, "Night at the beach is beautiful. Sometimes, when the moon is up, it shines on the sea so that it looks like a silver bridge all the way across the waves to the sand."

"Oh, I like that," Hibou said. "Well I'd like to come too. I'm good at seeing at night, even when there is no moon."

"That's very clever," I said. "I can't do that, but I can smell at night."

"I know," said Hérisson, holding his nose.

"Not like that," I said. "I meant I can smell what's going on everywhere around me."

"Just a little thought," Hibou said. "Do any of us know how we are going to get out of this place?"

We looked round. I thought that if Château Château had fallen down then all the walls would have fallen down too, but now that I was looking properly, I could see that they were all still there. It was just the castle that had fallen down.

I wondered if we could get out by the river. The only trouble with that was that the wheel was broken. It wasn't turning any more. We'd have to dive into the river, far, far down below. How safe was that? Not at all safe. Very, very dangerous in fact. All right for Hibou – she could fly. But Hérisson, Renard and me, we couldn't.

While we were talking, we hadn't seen that coming towards us was Chat. He was still dragging his box, but now he was carrying something with a cloth over it – another box perhaps? As he got near, he pulled back the cloth with a flourish and there was a cage, a birdcage.

We gathered round, looked in the cage and there was ...

Papillon! But oh dear, she wasn't flying about in the cage. She was lying on the bottom, very still.

"Oh no! Dear, dear Papillon," I said.

"All right, all right, I know this is bad," Chat said. "You see, I was trying to make her eat the flowers. I was so worried that I was going to lose my magic powers. I was … er … trying to force her. I'm sorry. Very, very sorry."

"And now look at her," I said, feeling myself beginning to cry.

"Is she dead?" Hibou asked.

We all got even closer. Then Hérisson said, "Hasn't this happened before? Isn't this what she does?"

I thought back to the time she flew so very high and then collapsed when she came down again. That time, she woke up, didn't she?

"I'm very, very, very sorry," Chat said again.

"Yes, you've said that before," Renard said crossly.

In the middle of this, guess who else turned up? Who had arrived so silently and smoothly that we hadn't heard her? Serpent!

"Anything wrong?" she said.

Chat screamed and jumped up on a rock close to us.

"It's you!" said Hérisson, thinking immediately (I thought) of that cellar.

"It's a snake!" Chat shouted. "Look out everybody."

No one moved.

"Are you crazy?" he said. "This could be the end of us. I didn't know there were snakes round here."

Serpent looked at him. "I was here long, long before you were, little cat. I was here in the time of the Ogre. I watched you play that clever trick on him, getting him to turn into a mouse."

"Mouse?" said Hibou, getting very interested in this story.

Serpent went on, "And I was here all through the time of the Marquis de Carabas and Princesse. I saw what you did to them. And I know what you did to all these poor creatures."

"I know," Chat said. "I am really so very, very sorry."

"What's more," Serpent said, "I can see poor Papillon is in trouble in that cage."

"Yes," Hibou said. "It looks like Papillon is ... she's ... she's..."

"I know what," Renard said. "Maybe she's starving hungry. We could put her on a flower and see if that helps?"

I tried to open the cage but it was locked. Chat put his hand to his belt, slipped the bunch of keys off, picked out one key and used it to open the cage.

"Sorry," he said. "I did lock her in. I told you I would turn out to be useful."

"Don't keep saying sorry," Renard said.

I reached in and picked up poor Papillon, and we looked round for some flowers. There were one or two little ones near by so I gently put her down on a yellow one. And we waited.

We waited and waited and waited.

Nothing.

"Hey!" Hérisson said. "What did you do last time she fell down flat like this?"

"I wagged my tail," I said.

"Well do it again, Gaston!" he shouted.

So that's what I did. I wagged my tail, wafted air towards

Papillon and then – just like before – first a ripple of the wings, then up on one leg, then up on two, then with another little flutter of the wings, our Papillon was back!

She buried her face deep into the flower, then took a long drink. After two or three of these, she had had enough. She picked her head up, looked round at us and said, "That was delicious. I haven't had anything to eat or drink for seven days and seven nights, you know, and I—"

She stopped herself, because she had just set eyes on Chat, the cruel cat who had kept her locked in a cage for a week.

Papillon hissed at him. "How dare you! How dare you stand there and look at me like that."

"I'm sorry, I'm really sorry," Chat said and coughed.

"Oh don't start him off again," Renard said. "We've had enough sorries to last us a year."

"Well," Papillon said very sunnily and brightly, "are we off to the seaside then?"

"Ye–es," I said, "but there is a bit of a problem."

"Problem?" Papillon said.

"Yes," I said, "we can't get out."

Our little band of friends went quiet. We were all getting excited, thinking that we were about to head off on the next part of our journey, but now we had reached another problem: how to get out. Were we stuck here for ever?

CHAPTER 12

In which we find
TREASURE!

"**I think** I may be able to help," Serpent said.

"Do you know a way out of here?" I said to her.

"Yes," Serpent said, "and—"

She was interrupted by Chat. "Impossible! There is no way out of Château Château."

"Impossible?" I said. "But didn't you say you wanted to come to the beach?"

"Oh yeah," said Chat. "Well, I thought as you lot are all so clever, you'd work it out."

Serpent took it slowly: "I told you, Chat, that I was here long, long before you. I know every inch and wrinkle of this place. I've been getting in and out for years."

"Hooray," shouted Hérisson.

"I know a little secret way that no one in the whole world knows but me."

"Impossible," said a bossy, buzzy voice.

Where did that come from? I thought. Chat had a little bag slung over his shoulder, and it popped open. It was Libellule. He had been in there all this time!

"Impossible for there to be a place here that I don't know of," Libellule said.

"Oh really?" Serpent said, looking cross. "You didn't even know that I existed."

At that, Libellule stopped buzzing. He even stopped shimmering.

Things were getting quite tetchy and cross between Serpent, Chat and Libellule now. What I wanted more than anything was to get out of this place.

"This way," Serpent said, and she started to head for a low circular stone wall.

"Ah yes," said Libellule, "the old water well. Of course. The way out. I knew that."

"No," Serpent said. "That was a trick."

She really is trying to prove a point, I thought.

We walked on past the old water well, towards where the old chapel once was. It was now a ruin; the roof had fallen in, so the pillars and columns were sticking up like lamp posts without lamps. Bits of stained glass lay all over the ground.

"Oh these are beautiful," Hérisson said, with his head very much DOWN.

"They are, aren't they?" Papillon said.

"Let's collect some," Hérisson said to her. "You pick them up and push them into my prickles and they'll stay there."

"Can we keep going?" I said. "Let's keep on following Serpent. She's going to help us get out of here."

We all followed after Serpent, most of us carefully tiptoeing round the broken glass so as not to cut our feet. Serpent headed over to what was left of the wall of the chapel. On it was a big stone with writing carved into it. She coiled up in front of it.

"Who can read this?" Serpent said. "Whoever can read the inscription will be able to open the stone. That's the way out, behind it. Read out loud what it says on the stone and you will see the way out..."

Hérisson shook his head. He couldn't read it. So did I. So did Renard and Hibou. Libellule shimmered. I think that meant he couldn't read it either. We all looked at Chat. He brushed some dust off one of his boots and coughed.

"Well, yes. As it happens, I can read it," he said, and moved nearer to the stone and the writing. There was a moment's quiet.

"And it says...?" Serpent asked him.

"Open sesame," Chat said.

"Nope," Serpent said.

"Open Cecily," Chat said.

"Nope," Serpent said.

"Open sausages," Chat said, beginning to sound desperate. He knew we were all looking at him. To think this great cat once ruled over us, and now he was not really much more than a kitten. I started to feel sorry for him, trying to prove to Serpent that he knew more than he did.

"What are we going to do, then?" I asked, because I really was getting desperate to get out of this place and on to the seaside.

Chat coughed. Maybe the cough was real. Maybe he really did have a bad chest, I thought. He slumped down on the ground next to his treasure box.

"Please tell us what it says," he said to Serpent.

"Yes," I said, "please tell us." And everyone else joined in.

~ CHAPTER 13 ~

In which we find that sometimes
you have to say goodbye.

Serpent looked hard at the writing on the stone and she started to chant:

"Wasco waxi in solo eff.
In solo eff wasco wax.
Waxi wasco eff in solo.
Eff in solo, lasco sax."

Nothing happened. So she said it again, this time closer to the stone.

"Shut your eyes, everyone, and say it with me:

"Wasco waxi in solo eff.
In solo eff wasco wax.
Waxi wasco eff in solo.
Eff in solo, lasco sax."

Just as we got to the end, we could hear the sound of stone moving over stone. We opened our eyes and, yes, the stone was moving. It swung open. And there behind it, we could see the top of a ladder going down.

Papillon whispered something in my ear. I pricked up my ears to hear her more clearly.

"That was nonsense," she whispered. "The stone opened because she pressed something in the floor."

I looked but I couldn't see anything. But then Serpent's coils were all over the floor anyway.

"There you are," Serpent said. "That's the way out."

"Of course it is," Libellule said, as if he knew all along. Serpent laughed.

We each stepped in through the opening: Renard, Hibou. Papillon flitting. Then Chat and Libellule. I heard Libellule buzzing.

I followed, expecting Serpent to follow me. But wait a moment: no Serpent.

"Don't you want to come, Serpent? After all you've done for us?"

The others popped their heads up out of the opening and looked at Serpent.

Serpent explained, "My place is here. I've been here for ever, I'll be here for evermore. The Ogre thought it was his, the Marquis and Princesse thought it was theirs, Chat thought it was his, but I was just waiting. I knew my time would come. Now there's me and my cellar and no one here to disturb me. I'm very sad to see you go. It was good to help you and break the magic power of that cat, but my place is here. My time has come."

Papillon and Hérisson were sad. I could see them bowing their heads so as to hide how sad they were. Me too. This was going to be a big goodbye for us. But sometimes there are goodbyes, I thought. After all, hadn't I said a big goodbye to my lovely friend, Hirondelle?

"Three things to remember," Serpent said. "One: don't listen to dead things. Don't do what they say. Second: on the Day of the Great Split, don't go the wrong way. Third: things aren't what they seem to be."

I wasn't sure that any of this was very helpful, but there we were, a little band of travellers, saying our goodbyes to Serpent.

Before heading down the ladder, I thought I'd take one last look at Serpent, so I popped back up. She was sliding off across the old chapel floor. I suppose I'll never see her again, I thought sadly.

Then I glanced down at where she had been lying coiled up. There was a metal button. I wondered ... was that the button that opened the stone?

Serpent looked back. I waved. She nodded and slid off into the rubble. I headed down the ladder after the others.

Now, surely, I thought, we'll be at the beach soon. I am so looking forward to it. Soon. Soon.

CHAPTER 14

In which we do some Big Thinking.

The ladder stretched down, down, down into the darkness.

"This is the way," Chat said.

"You don't really know, do you?" Renard said. "Is this a trick?"

"No," Chat said. "I want to get out of here as much as you do. Remember I started out as nothing more than a cat with a pair of boots, on the road. I want to get back to that simple life."

Libellule flew up. From the light of the shimmer of his wings, I could see a bit further.

"Hibou?" I said. "Does this look all right to you?"

Hibou peered into the dark. "Yes," she said, "all good."

I'll never know to this day what she could see that made her say that. I've always thought that she saw her favourite dinner down there, a mouse, or a rat.

"Let's carry on then!" I said. So one by one we climbed down the ladder, with Hibou and Papillon flying around us, and Libellule flying ahead of us, shining some shimmer so that we could see just a little.

Down, down, down we went till we got to the bottom. Down there was a little room.

"This is the sort of place where you'd expect to see worms," Hérisson said.

"Too deep for that," Renard said.

"How do you know?" said Chat.

"I just know that sort of thing," Renard said. "I'm a fox."

There was an entrance into a tunnel. Quite a small entrance, which we squeezed into and carried on walking. It was damp and earthy.

I was feeling good. After all our problems, we were on the road again. Everything was going to plan and there was quite a gang of us.

I went through them all in my mind: good little Hérisson, clever, brave Papillon, Renard – I was just getting to know her – and Hibou – she likes the night. There was no wise old Serpent with us any more of course, but there are always times you have to say goodbye, I thought. And not forgetting Chat and Libellule – hmmm, I really wasn't sure about them at all. Were we safe with them? Should we have left them behind? Mind you, there was the box ... the treasure box. There you go, Gaston, I said to myself, thinking about it again. Stop it! Don't think about it.

As I had that last thought, there was a rumbling sound, some loud thuds, a rush of air, and then a dense silence.

Hibou called out, "The tunnel's fallen in. We'll have to go back."

"OK," I said, "let's turn round carefully and head back."

We turned round, this time with me at the front. I took a few steps forward, back the way we came, when there was another rumble, some more loud thuds, that rush of air and the silence – a thick, cold silence.

We all realised what had happened. The tunnel had fallen in on both sides of us. The horror! We were trapped in a short passage of the tunnel. We were buried alive.

I was terrified. I got thinking.

"What are you doing?" Renard said.

"I'm thinking," I said.

"Why are your whiskers twitching?"

"That's what they do when I think," I said.

Renard took the lead. "Sit down everyone, and let's all have a Big Think."

"That's what I was thinking," I said, "thinking about thinking."

We sat down on the cold, damp earth. I was thinking as hard as I could.

Chat was whimpering like a kitten and jangling his keys. "We're trapped here. I need to get somewhere with my treasure. That's the point of treasure. You have to be somewhere nice to enjoy it. You can't eat it."

"Oh do stop whining," Renard said to him.

"He's not whining," Libellule said, "he's thinking out loud."

"And jangling his keys," I said.

"He's not jangling his keys," Libellule said. "They jangle all by themselves."

We had seen one of the keys open the cage that Papillon was in. What else could the keys open? I wondered.

Hérisson snorted. Of course he did.

"What now?" Renard said.

I heard Hérisson pattering his feet in the dark. "I've got an idea," he said. "I have friends."

"Yes, you do," Papillon said, "and it's wonderful that we've become friends so quickly."

"No," he said, "other friends."

"Well, please yourself," Papillon said, sounding a little hurt. I think she had rather hoped that Hérisson was going to give a little speech about how good we were all together in a gang.

Chat coughed.

"My other friends," Hérisson said, "may be able to help us." We all strained to hear what he was going to say next. "In the ground somewhere there are moles – taupes, as we say. Sometimes I do a bit of digging, but nothing like them. They can dig for miles, they can dig deep, dig long, dig fast, dig slow. They can dig, dig, dig, dig, dig, dig…"

"We get the point," Renard said, "they can dig. But how are we going to find any moles?"

"Ah well," Hérisson said, "you see when they're underground, moles talk to each other using a code. They scratch. It's the Scratch Code. *Scratch-scratch-scratch* means 'Hello'. *Scra-a-a-a-tch* means 'Worm!'. Did I say they like worms nearly as much as me? Well, they do and you see—"

"How is this scratch business going to help us?" Renard said.

"The thing is," Hérisson went on, "I know the Scratch Code."

CHAPTER 15

In which scratching comes
to be very important.

Hérisson started scratching. He scratched on the place where the tunnel first fell in. Then he scratched on the place where the tunnel fell in behind us.

We waited.

Nothing.

Then Hérisson scratched on the wall.

We waited.

Nothing.

This isn't going to work, I thought. It was a good idea. It was worth trying, but no. It's not going to work.

I could hear us breathing in the dark. Chat had started whimpering again. It really wasn't helpful whimpering either.

Then Hérisson scratched on the floor.

We waited.

Nothing.

"That's it," Hérisson said. "I've done what I can."

"And you were very good," Papillon said. "It was worth a try."

"Wait," Hibou said. "There's one place you haven't tried: the ceiling, the roof of the tunnel."

"I can't get up there," Hérisson said. "It's UP. I only ever really do DOWN."

"I could lift you up," Hibou said. "You climb on my back and I'll fly up there and you can get scratching."

"Hmm, I don't think it'll work," Hérisson said mournfully.

"Give it a try, Hérisson," I said. "Go on."

Hérisson climbed on to Hibou's back. Hibou took off and flew up towards the ceiling. Hérisson rolled on to his back and scratched away at the surface. *Scratch-scratch-scratch ... scratchety, scratchereeee, scritch...*

We waited.

Then came an earthy sound from up above us, and a bit of earth fell on the floor.

Hibou called out, "It's a mole! It's Taupe la Mole."

Chat stopped whimpering.

Hérisson explained to Taupe what had happened. He didn't need to use the Scratch Code now. "Is there any chance of a bit of help?" Hérisson asked.

Taupe thought about that. "Yes," he said, and disappeared.

"What's the use of that?" Chat said angrily. "He's gone. Some people are so thoughtless."

"How about you just hang on there?" Renard said.

So now we waited again. This time full of hope.

"Let's sing," Hibou said. "I know this sounds like boasting, but I have rather a good voice."

"No," Papillon said. "No singing. We have to save our breath in case the air runs out."

"Good point, Papillon," I said.

So we didn't sing. We just sat quietly in the dark. I tried to think very hard about the beach. The sea. The sand. It was my dream. And I was going to live that dream one day. Oh yes.

Then there was a very light thud. Followed by another. Then another.

Hibou called out, "Moles are falling from the ceiling."

She was right. One after another, moles were falling from the ceiling on to the floor. Five, ten, twenty, maybe as many as fifty. They seemed to know what to do straightaway because they all headed for where the tunnel had fallen in and got digging.

"Libellule," I said, "could you go and do some shimmering near where they're digging, so we can see them at work?"

"I suppose so," Libellule said rather reluctantly, but he did. He went off and did some shimmering right by the moles.

Dig, dig, dig, dig, they went at it, all fifty of them, till they had made a mini-tunnel through the earth in the main tunnel. The feeling of fresh air blew through to us. It felt cool and good.

"Well done, Hérisson," Renard said. "You've saved us."

Hérisson pointed at the moles.

"Oh yes, and thank YOU, moles," Renard said as politely as she could.

But they were off. It was like they didn't want to stay to be thanked. They had done their job. I figured that they just like digging, so when Hérisson got in touch with the Scratch Code, it sounded like another chance to do some serious digging. So they did. And that was that.

Us meanwhile: we started squeezing through the mini-tunnel one by one. It was quite smeary. The soil stuck to us but – no matter – we knew that this was saving us.

The next part of the tunnel wasn't so earthy. It was more chalky, a dull off-white that flickered in the light of Libellule's shimmer. We had only walked a few steps in this tunnel when we heard a voice. It was a beautiful voice, which, even though it was speaking, sounded as if it was singing.

"You've come," it said, "you've come at last."

It sounded so welcoming and kind.

"And you've come to the right place. The perfect place. For I can tell your ... fortune! I can see what will be. I know what will happen. I can read YOU!"

When it said that there was some kind of chorus of voices that joined in, saying, "Fortune! Fortune! Fortune! We can read YOU! We can read YOU!"

Oh, that sounded so sweet and so kind. I imagined hearing exactly what was going to happen to me, told in such a soft, loving way.

"And you will stay for ever..."

"And ever and ever..." came the chorus.

"Never leave..."

"Never ever leave..."

"Stay for ever and a day..."

"For ever and a day..."

The light in the tunnel had changed. It was as if someone had lit a special candle that shed a warm mauve light. The walls glowed and a light spicy smell wafted through.

"Oh I like this. I like this a lot," Chat murmured, and his keys jingled gently too.

"Me toooo," Libellule sang.

Hibou and Papillon sighed along with them.

But who was talking? Who was saying these things? Where was the chorus? And whose home were we in, where we were being made so welcome? It would be so lovely to meet them, I thought.

~ **CHAPTER 16** ~

In which I have a whole new thought.

Then I saw it.

On the wall, or rather, IN the wall, was a coil. A spiral. A bit like a snail but even more coiled. It was spinning slowly so that as I looked at it, and followed the spin, I felt my eyes go googly. Above, below and all round it in the wall I could see more beautiful stone coils, all spinning gently, all whispering and murmuring in chorus.

And these wondrous creatures could tell our fortunes? I realised straightaway they would be able to tell us whether we would get to the beach ... and what we would find when we got there. Again, the picture of the bright blue sky, the little wavelets running up the sand and slipping back again, the light wind on our faces... Would it really be like that? I so wanted to know. And these gorgeous kind creatures would tell me, tell all of us, tell all my new friends.

And I had another thought. A thought that I was only having now for the first time. It was to do with that box that Chat dragged around with him ... and that bunch of keys. What if, what if – I could hardly bear to say it to myself ... what if, at some time, that box became ... mine? And what if, what if, that bunch of keys became ... mine too?

What if I opened that box and in that box there were jewels and gold and silver, and it was all mine? With such treasure, I could surely have all that I would ever want for the rest of my days. But how? How could I get that box and those keys? Maybe these creatures could tell me if that was going to happen. I saw it clearly now, the spinning coil on the wall would know. Surely...

I stepped forward, closer to the first coil that spoke to us. I put my ear near to its dark, shiny surface.

Just then, I felt a hard, sharp tug. It was Renard. I turned.

How dare she? How dare she grab me like that, just as I was going to look into the future, see life as it was going to be, see whether the treasure was going to be mine.

I snarled and made my teeth look sharp and dangerous.

Renard wasn't worried. She just said, very calmly, "What did Serpent say?"

"I don't care what Serpent said," I answered furiously. "Serpent isn't with us. Serpent is yesterday. Serpent is just

some old snake stuck in a ruin, with her slugs and snails."

"And worms!" shouted Hérisson.

I looked round. And I saw everyone else – everyone, that is, apart from Hérisson – staring at their own coil on the wall. Their eyes were googly too. They were each getting closer and closer to the coils, hoping to hear more and more and more. The warm mauve light glowed and the spicy scent wafted through.

I looked at Hérisson. He wasn't looking UP at what was in the wall. He was looking DOWN.

"And worms!" he shouted.

This word broke something in my mind. I came out of the trance I was in. My dreams and hopes, my visions and images faded. The mauve faded. The scent turned sour. There was now just our raggedy, bedraggled gang standing in a muddy, chalky tunnel.

Hérisson had shattered the enchantment.

Renard smiled at me. "Serpent was right. Don't listen to dead things."

"Ah hah," I said, "these aren't stones in the walls, these are fossils..."

"Hmm," Hibou said, "that was her first warning. What was her second?"

I thought for a second or two. "It was ... er..."

I couldn't remember.

"Hey," I called out, "does anyone remember what Serpent's second warning was?"

No one could remember. So we walked on. Down the chalky tunnel.

After a bit, Hibou said to me, "What happened back there with those thingies on the wall?"

"What thingies?" I said.

"Back there," she said.

"Sorry," I said, "I don't remember. My mind ... er ... my mind is a bit fogged."

"Mine too," said Hibou.

"And mine," Chat interrupted.

"And mine," chipped in Libellule.

"And mine," added Papillon.

Somehow Renard hadn't been caught up in the mystery. I knew Hérisson hadn't, because of where he was looking. But how come Renard had dodged it? What was special about her? I always knew she was clever. Well, she was a fox after all.

As we walked on down the chalky tunnel I wondered about these things, and it felt like I was walking down a tunnel of mystery too.

CHAPTER 17

In which we are deep underground.

We plodded on. There was nothing else we could do. I must admit, my mind was becoming clogged. Perhaps it was the after-effect of the coils, perhaps it was because of a sense of hopelessness. It seemed that at every moment when we were getting to where we wanted to go, there was something in the way, something that stopped us. What next? I thought as we pushed on in the darkness, with the smell of damp earth and damp chalk in our nostrils.

Well, at least I had found some good friends, I thought. Maybe not quite as special as Hirondelle, but great friends all the same. Though I did worry about Chat. Was he a friend? Had he changed? And Libellule seemed to be Chat's eyes. I supposed that he had spent all that time in Château Château going out and about and reporting back to Chat. What's the word for that? Yes – spy! Libellule was Chat's spy.

Renard was leading the way. She had become some kind of chief.

"Hold it, everyone!" she called out. "We've come to the end."

The end? I thought. The end of a tunnel is when the tunnel ends. You come out of a tunnel into daylight. That's the end of a tunnel. What sort of end was this?

Renard answered my thoughts by banging on something. It made a big booming metal sound. We moved closer. Now we could feel and just about see that we had reached an iron barrier. The end of the tunnel was this. We were sealed in behind iron.

"Is it a door?" I said hopefully.

So we felt all over it, hoping to find a button or lever that would open it. But no. Nothing. This iron wall sat there, right in front of us: like a great big iron NO.

I felt all over the ground around us. Then I felt something that shocked me right through. And again. And again.

Bones.

Lying on the tunnel floor, half buried, I could feel the bones of travellers like us. Travellers who had got this far and couldn't get any further. They had walked and walked, got here and got stuck. Like us.

Is this what awaited us? Would we end up as nothing more than a pile of bones, picked over by worms and ants, woodlice, leatherjackets, dragged off by cockroaches and rats?

I thought I'd better keep quiet about this. No point in spreading fear round everyone. Keep quiet, I said to myself. At any other time, I might have thought, "Bones? Oooh, delicious bones!" But then and there, I was so horrified that I couldn't even think of having a chew on one.

"What if we banged on it?" Papillon interrupted my thoughts. "Though not much point in me trying to do that..." She laughed. "I could bang on it as hard as I tried and all that you'd hear is a little wisp of a sound. But if one of us could bang really loudly, maybe there's someone out there who'll hear and get us out. What do you think?"

We looked at each other. Who could make a noise? Hibou – she had a good strong beak. Hérisson – a bit of brushing with his prickles, though there were bits of stained glass stuck in them now. Libellule? No, much the same as Papillon. Me? Well, I could give it a go, I thought. I could have a go at pounding the iron with my paws. And Renard could do the same. That left Chat. Hmm, not much more than me or Renard. A bit of pounding with the paws. It didn't add up to much.

Then I thought of something else.

"I tell you what," I said, "there's one thing here that could make a big noise. If there's anyone out there they might hear it."

Everyone looked at me.

"The treasure box," I said. "We could whack that against this thing and create quite a racket."

Chat jumped on to the box. "No one, no one at all –" he coughed – "touches my box. This is mine. All mine. For ever mine."

"What do you suggest then?" said Renard with a slightly sneery voice.

Chat started to blather and bluster. "Well, there's ... I mean ... on the other hand ... in a general sort of a way ... I had in mind ... in the eventuality of..." He petered out.

Libellule tried to save him. "Chat is thinking."

Well, we could see that, but it wasn't getting him very far.

"Right," Renard said, "if none of us can think of anything else, and if we all think it would be a good idea to do something, then we use the box."

Chat was shocked and put his body round it, holding it like a drowning man clinging to bit of wood. But we weren't waiting. We knew it was this or nothing. So we grabbed the box, tugged it towards the metal barrier, pulling Chat with it. Then we lifted it up and used it like a big, square hammer to bash on the metal.

Bang! Bang! Bang! Bang! Bang!

I don't know how long we went on for but certainly for long enough to make us tired.

Just as we were beginning to flag, I heard a voice.

"All right, all right, I can hear you," it said. "I was just having a bit of a doze. My afternoon nap. What do you want?"

I shouted, "We want to get out! What do you think we want to do? Bake a cake?"

"Well, why don't you pull the rope?"

"What rope?" Hibou said. "It's dark in here but I can see more than the others, and there's no rope here."

"You won't be able to see it," the voice said.

"It's an invisible rope?" Papillon asked with an amazed voice.

"No, it's a dark rope," the voice said. "Spiders made it. You'll have to feel for it."

That got us searching all round for the feel of the kind of rope that a spider would make. Soon our eyes and noses were catching the faint wisps of spider webs, but nothing you could call a rope.

Papillon muttered, "I'm not absolutely sure I want to go looking for spiders' webs. Some of us get caught up in them and we don't ever get away."

I thought about the spiders in the barn back home and remembered seeing all sorts caught up in their webs: flies, wasps, moths and – yes – butterflies.

Chat and Libellule thought they'd sit it out too. They really weren't much help at all.

Hérisson, though, wondered if the rope went all the way down to the floor. If it did, he could snuffle along and find it.

I heard him grunting and snorting and snuffling about in the corner and sure enough, he was calling out, "Got it!"

He had found the thinnest strand of twisted spider web running down from the ceiling all the way to the floor where he was. Hibou could see it so she moved forward.

"Shall I?" she said.

We nodded. She pulled on the rope.

With a great creaking and grinding the big iron door – for that's what it was: a door – inched open, first letting in a sliver of light, then a whole ray, then a great rush of bright, bright sunlight, so bright that it hurt our eyes. We quickly shielded them and wandered outside.

It was hot. Very, very hot. Very, very, very hot.

By the time we could see properly, we could see each other, dirty, muddy, damp and shocked. Then we could see who the voice belonged to. Who was it?

CHAPTER 18

In which we come across
a different sort of treasure.

It was a yak. Yak le Yak.

A big hairy yak.

"Hello guys," he said in a dreamy, friendly sort of a way. "Welcome to out here!"

I looked round. We were by a river.

Papillon whooped. "This is the river!"

"Yes," I said.

"No." She whooped again. "The river I saw when I flew up into the sky and nearly died."

"I remember," said Hérisson.

I didn't think I did but that must have been the coils still working on me.

"And rivers go to the..." She was trying to get us all to join in. "To the...?"

Chat looked up. "The sea!" he said, and went back into his gloomy mood. He stroked his treasure box to comfort himself.

"Yes!" shouted Papillon. "All we have to do is follow the river to the sea."

"Yes," Renard said, "we can run along beside the river, along the riverbank. I'd like that."

Yak le Yak nodded his head towards the river. "Not much of a bank there, though," he said.

We looked. He was right. Instead of a bank there were two high cliffs. We had come out of the tunnel into a little open space just before the river plunged into a gorge, the water tumbling in white ripples and waves.

"I can't swim," Hérisson said straightaway.

"And I'm not much good at it," Chat said, but no one seemed to care.

Renard and I looked at each other. We both knew that we were quite good but this would be no help for the others.

What about this dreamy old Yak? Would he have some idea to help us? We hadn't really noticed something earlier: where the cliff jutted towards us, there was a cave. And round the cave was what at first sight looked like bits and piles of rubbish: logs, branches, old cans, metal bars, rope, broken dolls, wheels, bits of a pram, broken trolleys, part of a bike, heaps of old stuff.

"Hey, Yak," I said, "where does all this stuff come from?"

Yak said, "I collect it out of the water as it floats or rolls or tumbles past. People dump all their rubbish in the river upstream, down the river it comes and I collect it up. Kind of helps clean it up a bit."

It was a real mess. It made me think of my beautiful beach, stretching for miles and miles, pure white sand. No rubbish there.

"We're going to have to make a boat," I said. "Some sort of a raft."

Renard was sniffing around all over the bits and pieces that Yak had collected.

"Well, we've got all the stuff we need here," Renard said.

"Hold it right there," Yak said. The dreamy voice had gone. This was sharp. Even a bit cross. "No one touches my treasure."

"Treasure!" Chat snorted. "As if that's treasure!"

"I've spent years and years and years collecting these pieces," Yak said. "Each one has a history."

Well, yes, you could, if you looked hard, just about see that Yak had arranged his "treasure" – if that's what it was – in some sort of a way. Was that pile of white stones some sort of a picture, perhaps? But what was it a picture of? Were the logs arranged to look like a set of benches or some kind of castle?

"Most days, I sit with my treasure coming up with thoughts about where each thing came from," Yak said. "Like ... what it did when it was upstream from here. Who pushed that trolley? Who did that doll belong to? Who broke it and why? Were they angry?

"And I make up stories all day long. Sometimes that old teddy goes for a ride in the trolley in my mind. Sometimes the branches fly through the sky on a trip to other lands. They're treasures, you see. Anything can become anything. It's a good—"

"Argh!!!"

It was Chat. He had walked backwards to get out of the hot sun and had walked into – well – Yak did what he did wherever he was, if you get me. And Chat had stepped into it.

"Argh!" he called out again.

"Oh yeah, sorry," Yak said in his dreamy way. "Yeah, you see I'm here all on my own and I'm not too bothered about things like that. I just do it where I do it. I'm kinda free and easy, you see. You can go over to the water and give yourself a bit of a wash."

Chat was coughing and spitting, furious that he had made himself look so foolish. He dragged himself over to the water's edge, lugging his treasure box with him.

And I had that thought again: what would it be like to have those jewels and gold and silver all for myself?

"What's he got in that box?" Yak asked.

"Treasure, of course," Libellule said tetchily, and shimmered off to the water's edge to help with the washing-off.

"Mmm," Yak said, sounding doubtful. "Treasure? In one box? What sort of treasure is that?"

"Look," I said, "the thing is, we're trying to get to the sea. We need to make this raft thing. Do you think we could use some of your treasure to build a raft so that we can float down to the sea?"

Yak looked at us. "What can you give me in exchange?"

We all looked at each other. I guess some of us thought about Chat's treasure box, but there was not much chance of getting in there.

But just then, Yak looked a bit more closely at Hérisson. "I do like the beautiful pieces in your bristles. They would go so well with my treasures here."

Hérisson thought about that. He didn't seem to mind. I stepped in to make sure we had a deal. Perhaps I was thinking of Serpent and her deal about not treading on her.

"I tell you what," I said, "looking at those beautiful pieces, that Hérisson has carried for miles and miles, do you think there are enough for you to give us enough stuff to make a raft?"

Yak looked closely. "Mmm. The thing is," he said, "your kind of treasure never comes my way. You can see that. But each one of your treasures stuck on a log, sticking out of the end of an old tube, would make this place look like a palace."

Chat was still washing and when he heard this, he laughed. "Huh! Palace!" he said, and bent to smell his leg to see if he had managed to clean himself up properly.

I supposed if anyone knew about palaces, it was him. And Libellule.

"Huh! Palace!" Libellule repeated, taking Chat's side, as usual.

Papillon and Hibou picked and plucked the coloured bits of broken stained glass out of Hérisson's bristles and handed them over to Yak; while Renard and I got going with the logs and rope to make a raft. After a bit, I went over to Hérisson, who was sitting on his own.

"Are you sad to give up your stained glass treasures?" I said to him.

"Yes," he snuffled. "I wanted to take them back with me to my home near your barn and make a beautiful coloured trail with them."

"You've done a good thing, though," I said. "You've given them up so that we can have a raft. That's very kind."

"Hmm," he said more to himself than me, and went very quiet.

Yak stepped to and fro making sure all was fair, as he saw it. Libellule decided that this was a good time for a bit of sunbathing and Chat said that his cough was bothering him again. Yak sighed with delight now that he had these bright and beautiful new treasures to put on his old treasure.

"Ahhh!" we heard him sigh. And "Ooooh!" And "Ohhhh!"

Hérisson looked long and hard at Yak as he did so.

Suddenly, there was a dull, heavy humming sound. It was getting nearer and nearer and out of the corner of my eye I saw a small, yellow and black blur. A hornet was heading hard and fast for Chat le Cat.

I don't know what it had seen – or was it the smell that Chat had tried so hard to get rid of? Or perhaps the hornet was just on its usual route, the route it liked to go at this time of day.

"Duck," Yak said to Chat in a smiley sort of a way. "Let him through."

But Chat didn't duck. Perhaps Chat thought that Yak was telling him that there was a very small duck flying at him. In fact, it was something very large: a very large wasp, because that's what hornets are.

So the hornet flew straight into Chat and hit him with a *Voooop*!

This made two creatures angry: Chat for being hit, and the hornet for bumping his head. It hummed even harder.

Chat pushed the hornet, shouting, "Get off me!"

"Hey," Yak said, "no one should ever push a hornet. Pushing a hornet means trouble. Big trouble."

"Why's that?" Hérisson said.

"Harm one, harm them all," Yak said. "That's hornet truth. Wait and see."

Yak was right. In what seemed no more time than it takes to squeeze a lemon, hundreds of hornets appeared out of Yak's cave and homed in on Chat.

"Jump in the river!" Yak shouted.

Chat knew that a hornet cloud really did mean bother. Still pulling his treasure box, he jumped into the water, leaving the box on the edge, attached to his belt by the rope. Under the water he went.

The cloud of hornets swooped towards the water with an angry howl ... but, you see, hornets can't swim, so they weren't going to dive in after Chat. And Chat kept all of

himself under the water for as long as he could. Just once, I caught sight of the very tippy tip of his nose coming up for air, but it quickly disappeared out of sight again.

The hornets soon got fed up chasing nothing more than a ripple in the water. They gathered up their friend, and roared back where they came from. And where was that? Yak's cave. Did he really live with hornets? I wondered.

Chat came out of the water, hissing at his wet fur. "I hate wet. I hate wet."

Yak was laughing. "Like I said, hornets live by a great rule: harm one, harm all. You harm one hornet, all the rest will rush to help the hornet in trouble."

Chat shook and trembled and shivered, partly because he was cold and partly because he was angry. He had never lived by this rule, so he wasn't going to enjoy it that hornets did. He hissed again.

Meanwhile we had to get on making a raft that was big enough for Hérisson, Renard, Chat and me. Hibou, Papillon and Libellule could fly along above us, looking ahead to see what was coming up. And this way we could paddle and float all the way to the sea.

Oh, we were so nearly there!

Or were we?

CHAPTER 19

In which we set sail.

The raft was done.

Yak stood at the side of the water, ready to push us off.

"I'm sorry to see you go," he said, with his dreamy voice sounding quite sad now. "I don't get to see many people."

"Right, Yak," Renard called out, "give us a shove!"

And he did! We were away, off on the fast-running river water.

"Oh," Yak called after us, "don't forget the Great Split!"

"The what?" I shouted as we moved off faster and faster, picked up by the power of the flow.

I didn't catch what Yak said next as the roar of the current was too loud.

Great Split? I thought. What's that? There was some faint echo in my mind of something that Serpent said to us … but no, I couldn't quite remember it. And if I couldn't remember it, it can't have been too important, I thought. I looked at the others – Renard, Hérisson, Chat – all settling into places on the raft, with Hibou, Papillon and Libellule flying above us.

It was pacy, it was rough, but it was exciting. We were moving at speed. The cliffs on either side were a blur. We're going to get to the sea pretty quickly at this rate, I thought. There was a delicious freshness in the air. The wind off the water was blowing in our hair and I could see in the light of the others' eyes that they were hopeful and happy for the first time in some time.

All but Chat, who was straightaway starting to look queasy. The rocking of the raft was getting to him and his eyes were rolling round and round.

"LOOK OUT!" shouted Papillon, who was flying ahead of us.

"YES, LOOK OUT!" Hibou called too.

Then we saw it: up ahead, in the middle of the river, was something that looked like a giant blade, a gigantic knife standing tall, high as the cliffs; tall, tall in the water, with its cutting edge facing directly at us. The running rapids rushed on either side of it, foaming around its base.

We would have to choose one side or the other. If not, we would be sliced in two. But could we steer the raft down the right or the left channel? Or were we plunging helplessly towards the gigantic blade? Didn't Serpent say, "Don't go the wrong way?" But which way was the wrong way, and which way was the right way?

CHAPTER 20

In which I have selfish thoughts.

"**W**e're going LEFT!" Renard shouted. Without thinking about it, we moved to the left side of the raft. Well, Renard, Hérisson and I did. Chat stayed right, leaning over the edge in case his stomach was going to give him problems.

Nearer and nearer we rushed towards the great blade. Were we going to whoosh down the left channel, or were we going to hit the blade? The water was rushing so fast, we were out of control. There was nothing we could do. We just didn't have the power to change it. The water was in charge.

I shut my eyes. I could hear the rush of the water. I could feel the spray on my face. I held my breath. Left, left, left, I thought, wishing for the best.

But then came the hard, loud noise of a giant axe going through wood. Just once. And then the rushing sound once more.

I opened my eyes. We were in a narrow channel, moving a bit more slowly now. I looked round. What had happened? The giant blade had sliced our raft. Not in half, but it had sliced off one side of it. Was anyone hurt?

Here we all were, Renard, Hérisson and me, with Papillon, Hibou and Libellule up above. That was good. Oh! Hang on, where was Chat? Oh no, he had been on the right-hand side of the raft! The blade had sliced the right-hand side of the raft off with him on it.

"We've lost Chat!" I shouted. "We've lost Chat!"

The others looked round. They were shocked too. None so shocked as Libellule.

He cried out, "Oh no, oh no!" and swooped down to the raft to sit beside us. No matter what we thought of Chat – and some of it wasn't very nice – we could see that Libellule was desperately sad. He was devastated. He sat on a piece of rope and cried, long and hard. Hérisson sat down next to him, and made kind snuffly noises.

I thought of the hornets' rule: "Harm one, harm all." Here was a way, I thought, that Chat being harmed had harmed us. Only ... only ... we hadn't been able to help him. And now our gang was hurt. Libellule was wrecked with sorrow. We all sat quietly thinking about how Libellule was feeling, thinking of people we had lost.

For a moment, I thought of old Serpent and how we had left her behind in the rubble of Château Château. If only she had come with us, maybe we could have done something to get the raft down the left channel with all of us on it, safe and sound. What was her second rule? Yes, I remembered: "Don't go the wrong way." But had we gone the wrong way? Or had Chat gone the wrong way?

But that was in the past now. And I realised you can't do anything about the past. All you can do is learn from it. And perhaps I was learning something. But what?

The river was becoming calmer. It was a bit wider and deeper so the white tops had sunk. The sun was up in the sky, but the cool of the water reached us too. We relaxed and waited. Surely now we were nearly at the sea. What a story I would have to tell Hirondelle when we get back, I thought. She would be amazed.

I looked over to Libellule again. Then I noticed something. The great blade had sliced through everything, even the rope between Chat and the treasure box. Chat was gone, but the treasure box was on the raft. With us.

I stared at it. Could it really be that the treasure was ... ours? I stared at it some more. What if ... what if ... what if the treasure box was ... mine? Just mine?

Yes, that greedy, selfish thought washed over me like a shower of warm water. I bathed in the dream of all those jewels and gold and silver that I imagined were in the treasure box. All mine. With that I could have whatever I wanted. Anything at all.

I dozed off, into a lovely hazy, lazy sleep. A sweet, sweet sleep full of dreams of richness.

~ CHAPTER 21 ~

In which we hear about the Palace of Dreams.

"**C**heckpoint! Checkpoint!"

What was that noise? Who was shouting?

It was Hibou and Papillon. They had seen something coming up. I opened my eyes. Ahead of us was a kind of gate, spanning the whole river. We would float straight into it.

At one side was a hut. Renard was paddling, now that the water was slow, and she took the raft over to it. On the side of the hut was what looked like a speaker. A voice came out of it. "Take your ticket," the voice said, "and the gate will open."

What's the point of that? I thought.

Then the voice went on: "You are coming to the Palace of Dreams. Take your ticket. Pay at the péage on the way out, or you will have to stay in the Palace of Dreams. Take your ticket and the gate will open."

"The Palace of Dreams?" Hérisson looked up. "That sounds great. Take the ticket!"

He said this because he couldn't reach up to take the ticket himself. It was sticking out of a slot on the wall next to the speaker. I reached up and took it.

The gate opened and Renard paddled us through. The gate closed behind us.

"What's a 'péage'?" Hibou said.

"It's a thing where you pay to go through," Renard explained.

"But we've gone through," Hérisson said, "and we didn't pay."

"No," Renard continued, "we pay at the other end."

"What other end?" said Hérisson.

"The other end of the Palace of Dreams," Renard said. "There'll be a gate. When we pay, that gate will open."

Hérisson thought about that. Then he started up again. "What do they want money for?"

"Well," Renard said, "I'm not totally sure but I guess that'll be to pay to keep the Palace of Dreams going ... all the stuff in the Palace of Dreams."

"Hmm," Hérisson said.

"Yes, that must be right," Papillon said. "I like dreams."

"Me too," said Hibou.

Libellule was still too sad to think about it.

Where is this palace? I thought. And the moment I thought it, I felt the raft speed up. The water beneath us felt as if it had a bit more of a current. Stronger and stronger flowed the current and faster and faster went the raft.

Libellule looked up, took off with a bit of his shimmer coming back, moved ahead, turned and came back.

"It's a waterfall. We're going over a waterfall."

A waterfall? A great flowing wall of water, rushing down to foaming froth below? We were in trouble now. We would be hurled from the raft, thrown into the water, smashed to pieces!

Still the raft sped up. Faster and faster. Now I could see ahead how the water seemed to come to an edge, with nothing beyond. A line on the surface of the water, where the whole river tipped over the edge of a cliff.

This was the Palace of Dreams? Some palace! (Now where had I heard that before?)

"Everyone hold tight on to the raft," shouted Renard. "The raft will save us. Believe in the raft."

Hibou, Papillon and Libellule looked on, unable to help, just hoping for the best.

And then over we went with a great lurch.

It felt as if my stomach was being flung up into my mouth. I held on as tight as I could. I looked across to Renard and Hérisson. Renard was fine, but Hérisson was wobbling. The world was spinning round. The water was in the sky. The sky was in the water. I grabbed Hérisson and held him tight too.

We clung on like that for what seemed like a lifetime. We were flying down, down, down, but not through wind and air – through water. White water was all around us ... until – *SPLOOSH!*

We crashed into the foam at the bottom, and down we went into the swirling water, spinning and turning.

But it was a good raft, a raft that floated well, and soon it was climbing back up, through the streams of bubbles and whirling currents. We burst to the surface, away from the waterfall. I looked back. There it was, that wall of white water! And we had just come down that! Us on our little raft, and we were all still here. We had done it!

Hibou, Papillon and Libellule cheered. "You did it! You did it!"

Hérisson crept out from under me. "Thank you, Gaston," he snuffled, "thanks a lot. So was that the Palace of Dreams?" he continued. "Didn't feel much like a palace and the only thing I was dreaming about was, 'when will this end?'"

That was one of Hérisson's jokes. It cheered me up. But he was right. Where was the palace?

CHAPTER 22

In which we think: what is treasure?

The river calmed down. We floated gently towards an archway. It looked like the entrance to Yak's cave. Surely we weren't back there?

No, this was a new cave. We floated into a huge, high hall, lined with crystals that glimmered in the half-light. Down from the ceiling came glistening pillars, reaching down to more pillars that pointed upwards. The whole scene was silvery. The river was quiet, but if you craned your ears you could hear a soft dripping. The drips were falling from the pillars: *plip, plip, plip, plip*. But as many, many pillars dripped and the pillars were all of different sizes, each plip was a different note from the next. I listened. They were playing a tune ... or was it a song? Was this great hall telling us something? Was it in a language I didn't know?

On and on it went, a lovely soothing sound, and before I knew it, pictures were floating into my mind. First I saw Hirondelle. Waiting for me to come back. She looked lonely. She sat on the edge of the barn roof, looking and looking.

And I wasn't there. She hung her head down, wondering and wondering. I wanted to reach out and say, I'm here! I'm nearly at the beach. And then I'll be back. Not long now. But I couldn't because it was just a picture. A vision. And then the vision faded and I was back in the high hall, lulled by that lovely sound of the droplets falling from the pillars and into the still water.

As I listened, another vision came to me: the jewels, the gold and silver in the treasure box. They shone and twinkled in my eye. But then behind them came the Ogre – a ghastly, toothy creature with angry eyes, claws at the ready, as if the whole world was his enemy. He was leaning over the treasure, snarling at whoever he could see. Then he snapped the lid shut and leered around the room.

My vision followed him to a city, to a street of tiny shops: inside them were squirrels, poring over jewels – diamonds, rubies, sapphires – and pieces of gold and silver. The squirrels were cutting and polishing and grinding, turning rough stones into special shapes full of angles, or pressing gold into rings, silver into cups. They didn't stop, on and on, faster and faster, and then in came the Ogre. He leered and roared, snapped his teeth, and scratched his claws on the walls. Then he leaned over the squirrels, pulled them out of the way, lifted them up by their tails and flung them across their workshops into the corners, where they whimpered and grizzled. Then he grabbed the jewels and rings and silver cups, stuffed them into a filthy bag, roared his horrible leery laugh and left.

Again my vision followed him back to his treasure box. His great paws fingered the box, his claw found a catch, the lid flipped open and he poured everything he had seized from the squirrels into the box, and he slammed it shut. Then he sat on the box and laughed a great hollow leery laugh that woke me out of my vision. The laugh echoed through the hall long after I woke from the dream. And the first thing that came into my mind was Serpent's third warning: "Things aren't what they seem..."

I was left thinking about how the Ogre had stolen all that stuff. And then how Chat le Cat had eaten the Ogre and got the treasure, and now that Chat had gone, it was ours. But was it? Was it really ours? Or did it belong to the squirrels? Wasn't it them who had done all that work to make the treasure so lovely and lustrous? And I thought how I had dreamed of having it all for myself. Was that right? I asked myself. Was that fair?

In the middle of this thinking, our raft reached another checkpoint, another gate across an arch at the end of the high hall. I could see light through the bars in the gate. I could see something... Was it the yellow of some sand? And beyond that, was it the blue of the sea? It was! We were here! We had arrived. All we had to do now was pay at the péage, the gate would open and we would be there.

There was a speaker again.

"Put your ticket in the slot," said the voice.

"Who's got the ticket?" I said.

"You have," said Papillon.

"I haven't got it," I said.

"You've got it," said Renard to Hérisson.

"No, you've got it," said Hérisson to Renard.

"I haven't got it," said Hibou.

"I haven't got it," said Libellule.

"Where's the ticket?"

Hérisson snorted, "It's here!"

He was of course looking DOWN, and he had found the ticket jammed between two logs in the raft.

"Great!" Renard said, took it off him and pushed it into the slot.

The voice said, "Pay with your card."

We haven't got a card, I thought. I leaned over to the speaker. "We haven't got a card."

The voice said, "What have you got?"

I looked around. There was just the logs of the raft and the rags we were wearing, worn out and dirty from all we had been through to get here.

"Nothing," I said.

The voice came back, "What about that box?"

What was the voice talking about? I looked again. Oh yes, the treasure box. Of course.

"The treasure box, you mean?" I said.

Renard hissed, "Shh, keep quiet about that. It's ours. Don't give it away."

"Yes," Hérisson said, and all the others joined in.

It was at that moment that I knew something: all the others had had thoughts like my thoughts, that they could each get that treasure all for themselves. But no one had said. Who knows what thoughts they had had about how to get that treasure away from the rest of us? We had each longed for it, thought about how to get it and keep it.

I was sorry that the treasure had made us think like that. Then I thought, no, it wasn't the treasure that made us think like that. It was us. Treasure is just treasure, sitting doing nothing. We had done this to ourselves.

"The box," said the voice. "What's in it?"

And to tell the truth, none of us knew.

So, I said, "I don't know."

"Then open it," the voice said sternly.

But how? There was a keyhole on the side, but where was the key?

"Libellule?" Renard asked. "Where's the key?"

Libellule came back straightaway with, "On the bunch of keys on the belt that Chat is wearing."

At that moment we realised we couldn't open the box.

The voice said, "If you can't open the box and give me something, I can't open the gate."

We were stuck again. And maddeningly and infuriatingly, just over there was the beautiful beach, the soft sand, the endless blue sky. My dream! But we were no nearer to it now than when I was sitting back in the barn talking to Hirondelle about it.

Then I remembered my vision. I reminded myself of what the Ogre did to open the treasure box. Didn't he find some little catch that made the lid spring open?

I moved nearer to the box and looked at it. But something stopped me. Maybe I should pretend that I too didn't know how to open it. Then, if by luck or chance the voice let us through, at some point, maybe in the middle of the night, I could creep over to the box and get all the treasure for myself! Yes!

But no. If I did nothing and we sat here for hours and hours, days and days, weeks and weeks, I would be being cruel to my friends, hurting them, harming them all because I wanted the jewels and gold and silver for myself. I saw in my mind's eye all of us sitting right here, on the raft, nothing to eat, getting weaker and weaker, all because I wouldn't say that I knew how to open the box.

I thought about the hornets' rule: "Harm one, harm all." And here was me doing the opposite: "All for me and harm for all." And I felt ashamed of myself.

I moved closer to the box. I imagined myself as the Ogre, fingering the box. And as I ran over the bumps and dips in its surface, my paw caught on the tiniest of little bars, hidden behind a bolt. I pulled it and *CLICK!* The lid of the box flew open.

"Wow!" Hibou said. "How did you do that? That was like me seeing things in the dark."

"Things aren't what they seem," I said.

Hibou wasn't listening. Even I had stopped listening to what I was saying, because now we were all staring at what was inside the box. We had been right all along. It was full

of diamonds, rubies, sapphires, gold rings and tiny silver cups and chains.

The voice called out, "Thank you! Diamonds first."

No one moved. No one wanted to hand over anything.

"Then I don't open the gate."

Still no one moved.

"Look," I said, "you know it's not really ours. This stuff. It's not ours."

"Quite!" Libellule said sharply. "It belongs to Chat."

"Well, Chat isn't here," Renard said.

"Hang on," I said, "it didn't belong to Chat either."

"Oh yes it did," said Libellule.

"No," I said, "Chat stole it from the Ogre by eating him."

Libellule shimmered angrily.

"Well if Chat ate the Ogre, and we can't find the Ogre, it belongs to me – I mean – us," Renard said, pleased that she had got it sorted.

"No," I said. "Who do you think carved and polished the jewels, made the rings and cups and chains?"

We didn't know. I didn't even know if the squirrels really existed. It was just a vision.

"And who dug the diamonds and rubies and sapphires

and gold and silver out of the ground?" Hérisson said, enjoying it that such beautiful things came from DOWN.

We stared at the treasure, amazed that all that work had gone into making them so beautiful. We knew what we had to do.

"Diamonds first," said the voice again, and Renard stepped forward, picked up some diamonds and put them in the bucket that was set into the wall next to the speaker. There was a clicking, clacking sound as if something deep down in the bucket was counting and checking.

"Next," said the voice.

So Renard picked up some more jewels and tossed them in.

More clicking and clacking.

"Next," said the voice.

"Hey," Papillon said, "all this just to get a gate to open?"

"Next," said the voice.

In went the gold rings. Now all that was left were the little silver cups and the chains.

"Next," said the voice.

And so it went on till the treasure box was empty. Nothing left. Well, I thought, at least it meant that none of us would have those horrible thoughts about how to get the treasure for themselves, how to cheat the others or how to trick anyone.

"And the chain you're hiding," said the voice.

We looked at each other. Who had the chain?

Do you know who it was?

Me.

I know. I didn't say. But you see, I knew a little trick, where it looks like you're passing something to someone else but really you're hiding something at the same time. I had done that. And here I was, shown up in front of everyone else.

But how did the voice know?

"Sorry," I said to everyone, realising what a bad thing I had done. I tossed the silver chain into the bucket.

"Thank you," said the voice.

Hérisson muttered something to me. I leaned closer. "It's all right Gaston. No need to say sorry. I would have done the same thing myself."

And the others nodded. I felt better.

There was a pause and then bit by bit the gate opened.

We whooped and cheered. We paddled the boat out of the cave and there in the distance ahead of us was ... the beach!

We had arrived!

But, but – who was here?

CHAPTER 23

In which we are amazed.

Hirondelle!

Yes, there, by the side of the river as it splayed out, finishing its long journey from way back in the hills, was Hirondelle.

"Hirondelle!" I called out to her. "You're here. How did ... how did you get ... but ... you were there, back there in the barn!"

"I flew," she said. "I'm a traveller, you know."

"Are you?" I said. "How do you travel?"

"I fly," she said. "It's what I do."

"But Hirondelle," I said, "I've got so much to tell you. We have had so many adventures."

"Me too," said Hirondelle, "I've got a lot to tell you. I don't know if I'll have time to get through it all, because, you know, it's getting to be time soon that I move on."

"Is it?" I said. "We've only just met up again."

"Yes," she said, "but I've got thousands of miles further to go."

I felt a bit sad that after all this journey and adventure, we wouldn't be together for very long. Hirondelle saw me

looking sad and said, "But I'll be
back."

"Oh good," I said, "and while
you're still here, before you go, do
you want to meet my friends?"

I waved to them on the raft and they all came over and
met Hirondelle.

"Phewwwww!" That was Hérisson. He was panting. It
was too hot for him. Now that he had said that, I thought it
was hot too. Soon we were all saying how hot it was. Much
hotter than how I remembered it. And there was no breeze
coming off the sea to cool us down. I looked around for some
shade. Hadn't there been some trees, where the light played
with the shadows thrown by the leaves?

No, there were no trees. There were some burnt-out
stumps. It looked as if there had been a fire here. A forest fire
that had burned away the trees that had fringed the beach.

I thought maybe we should dive into the sea and try to
cool down that way.

"Come on!" I shouted. "Let's go for a swim!"

That was good for Renard. Not so good for Hibou, Papillon
and Libellule. And not so good for Hérisson either.

"I'll go to the hut over there," Hérisson said. "It looks
like there's some space underneath it, that might be cooler."

"Me too," said Hibou. "I can't wait till it's night. Maybe
it'll be cooler then."

Papillon and Libellule didn't mind the heat so much, and while no one had noticed they had worked out some kind of mid-air dance where Papillon flitted to and fro and Libellule shimmered. Well, he always shimmered but there was some special kind of shimmering going on there.

So Renard and I ran to the sea.

"Come and watch us, Hirondelle!" I shouted.

"No, I'll go and perch on the side of that hut," she said. "That suits me."

The sand was baking hot. It burned our feet and then, when we got to the water's edge, we stopped. The foam that licked the sand was brown and greasy. I could see bits floating in it.

I couldn't tell what sort of bits. Bits of stuff. I looked down the beach. Where I had seen in my mind an everlasting strip of sand, white in the sun, being gently watered by the waves, it now looked flecked with rubbish. Bits and more bits of stuff. Not the kind of stuff that Yak had turned into his museum. Much smaller than that. And useless.

I looked again at the foam. It wasn't good.

"Are we going in there?" I said to Renard. "It's not how I remember it."

"I don't think so," Renard said. "I think I'll give it a miss. Is this really what we've come for? All this long way, and this is it?"

"It's changed, Renard," I said. "It's not how I remember it at all."

So we turned back and followed the others to the hut. Hérisson was snuffling around underneath it. I could guess what he was looking for, but then even under the hut it was dry and I knew that worms don't like dry earth one little bit.

Hirondelle was up on the edge of the roof, cheeping quietly to herself, looking out over the ocean. I couldn't see where Hibou was. Perhaps she had gone inside. So I knocked on the door.

"Come in," said a woman's voice.

CHAPTER 24

In which I meet two strangers from long ago.

I pushed the door open, and though it was dark and just a bit cooler inside, I could make out two people. A man and a woman. They were sitting at a table, sipping water.

"Who are you?" they said.

"I'm Gaston le Dog," I said, "and you?"

"I'm Princesse," said the woman.

I took in a deep breath.

"Let me guess," I said to the man, "you are the Marquis."

He laughed. "I used to be. But before that I was the miller's son."

"Oh yes," called out Hibou from where she was sitting in the corner. "I was right, it's the Puss in Boots story!"

"So what are you now?" I asked.

"I'm me. Dave. Someone who I want to be. Not someone who a miller wants to be better than I am. Not someone made into something I never was, by a cat."

"And are you really Princesse?" I said to the woman.

"Again. Not really any more. I'm Aisha. We just live here, where we are on the edge of the world. I don't want to be what others want me to be either," she said. "My parents wanted me to marry a king and look at me: I'm with Dave on the edge of the world."

"Did you go round on the mill-wheel, hold your breath and swim away from Château Château?" I said.

"How did you know?" Aisha said.

"I figured it out from what Serpent told me," I said.

"Who's Serpent?" Dave said.

I told them the whole story of Serpent and the secret life she led in Château Château, how she helped us, what she told us and how, sad to say, we left her there. And her three warnings...

"Don't listen to dead things. Don't do what they say.

"Second: on the Day of the Great Split. Don't go the wrong way.

"Third: things aren't what they seem to be."

They were amazed.

"Did you go the wrong way or the right way?" Aisha asked me.

I said, "Well, if we're here, I suppose it could be the right way. I'm not sure. I mean, if it was the wrong way, we wouldn't be here, would we?"

"Mmmm," Aisha said, not really very sure what I was talking about.

"What do you do all day?" Hibou said.

"We clean up stuff," Aisha said. "It feels like this place is where all the junk and muck in the world comes. And we clean it up..."

There was a scratching sound coming from underneath the hut.

"That's Hérisson," I said. "I made friends with him right at the start of this journey. It's good to have friends, isn't it?"

"Yes, it is," Aisha said, looking into Dave's eyes. But Dave wasn't looking back. He was looking at the door with complete shock and horror.

We turned to see what he had seen.

It was Chat.

There he stood, battered and worn out, as if one leg was

longer than another, his tail drooping, his ears drooping, his eyes drooping, his fur looking sticky and dirty.

"Hi," he said quietly and mournfully, "it's me."

"You went down the right channel," I said, not thinking that he knew that anyway.

"Yes," he said, "it was tough going. I ... no, I'll tell you later. It wasn't good."

"But you got here," I said, feeling a little bit sorry for him.

Chat looked at Dave and Aisha. "Look," he said, "I'm so sorry. I'm so, so, so, so—"

"No!" Aisha said. "In a strange way, you saved us. We were stuck in that palace, being horrible people, stuck up, vain, crazy about looking fancy, spending money, making people slave away for us."

"Oh well," Chat said, "glad to see that some good came of it. You know," he turned to me, "when the raft hit that giant blade, I got separated from my treasure box. Did it ... did it travel with you guys?"

"Yes," I said, "it did. It's over there on the raft. If..."

I didn't have to go on. Bruised and tired as he was, Chat picked himself up and rushed across the beach to the raft, and fell on to his treasure box, roaring, "Mine, mine, all mine!"

He pulled his bunch of keys from his belt, slotted the key into the lock and very slowly the lid opened. Hah! As if he didn't know the trick with the secret button!

By now, we had all caught up with him and were standing (or flying) round him, watching. As the box opened, Chat looked in and saw to his amazement and horror that it was ... empty!

He turned on us and yelled, "You stole it! You stole my

treasure! You … you…" He was trying to think of terrible names to call us.

"Where did you get it from?" Aisha asked.

Chat simmered down a bit. "All right, all right, I got it from the Ogre."

"Where did the Ogre get it from?" I said.

"I don't know!" Chat screamed.

Hirondelle was swooping to and fro over us all. Catching flies, I thought. Just like the old days.

"Hey, Chat," she said, "there's always treasure somewhere, you know. It might be right in front of you – here!" And as she said, "Here!" she circled round over us.

"You mean," I said, "us! We are a treasure. Us, the gang! Friends. Helping each other!"

"And there's another treasure," Hirondelle said. "Well, it was here, and over there, and in all the places we've been, and in all the places we haven't been. Our world. There's no bigger treasure than our world. I'll soon be off on my long, long journey, travelling on, to see how we're looking after that treasure. The whole here-and-there of everywhere. If we don't look after it, we won't have it any more."

At that, she circled once more, and then flew up into the sky, where she joined hundreds more like her, and slowly the great cloud of house martins and swallows made off into the distance.

"You'd all better come back to the hut," Dave said, "or we'll fry out here."

"Good idea," I said, and we ran back to Dave and Aisha's hut. They even let Chat come too, so long as he cleaned himself up first. There was still some clear cool water from a spring at the back of the hut.

We all drank a lot of that.

And as we sat there drinking that lovely cool water, I thought, we may have come to the end of our journey but we've still got a lot of work to do here ... together!

Yes, we'll do it together, I thought.